KIN
Rooted in Hope

Carole Boston Weatherford

ART BY

Jeffery Boston Weatherford

Atheneum Books for Young Readers

New York London Toronto Sydney New Delhi

A
atheneum

ATHENEUM BOOKS FOR YOUNG READERS

An imprint of Simon & Schuster Children's Publishing Division

1230 Avenue of the Americas, New York, New York 10020

Text © 2023 by Carole Boston Weatherford

Jacket illustration © 2023 by Jeffery Boston Weatherford

Jacket design by Greg Stadnyk © 2023 by Simon & Schuster, Inc.

Interior illustration © 2023 by Jeffery Boston Weatherford

ATHENEUM BOOKS FOR YOUNG READERS is a registered trademark of Simon & Schuster, Inc. Atheneum logo is a trademark of Simon & Schuster, Inc.

For information about special discounts for bulk purchases, please contact Simon & Schuster Special Sales at 1-866-506-1949 or business@simonandschuster.com.

The Simon & Schuster Speakers Bureau can bring authors to your live event. For more information or to book an event, contact the Simon & Schuster Speakers Bureau at 1-866-248-3049 or visit our website at www.simonspeakers.com.

Interior design by Irene Metaxatos

The text for this book was set in Caslon Antique.

The illustrations for this book were rendered in scratchboard and digitally.

Manufactured in China

0523 SCP

First Edition

10 9 8 7 6 5 4 3 2 1

CIP data for this book is available from the Library of Congress.

ISBN 9781665913621

ISBN 9781665913645 (ebook)

TO THE ANCESTORS WHO
CARRIED US THROUGH AND THE
GENERATIONS THAT WILL CARRY
ON. IN HONOR OF MY PARENTS,
JOE AND CAROLYN.

—C. B. W.

TO MY ANCESTORS AND EVERYONE
WHO FOUGHT FORWARD THROUGH
ALL ADVERSITY TOWARD THE
HOPE OF A BETTER FUTURE.
AND TO MY WIFE, WHO
ENCOURAGES ME CONSTANTLY
TO DO THE SAME.

—J. B. W.

Before Alex Haley's novel *Roots*
proved otherwise, few Black people
thought it possible to trace ancestry
beyond the cold heart of enslavement
to the warm sun of Africa.

Some dogged descendants dared the quest.

But my teenage self was more concerned
about the coming weekend than the past.
I learned of Frederick Douglass in social studies.
But I knew of only one enslaved ancestor,
my great-great-grandfather Phillip Moaney,
whose black-and-white oval portrait—
notable for a bushy mustache—
hung in the parlor of our century-old farmhouse.

There, I was grounded in rural villages
planted by long-gone relatives,
now resting in church graveyards.
Land memory sown in my searching soul.
Glory, the film about the first Black regiment
in the Civil War, won Denzel Washington
the first of his Academy Awards:
Lord. Lord, Lord, Lord. I had no inkling
that my own great-great-grandfather,
Isaac Copper, served in the U.S. Colored Troops.

What did a nineteen-year-old know?
I knew—after eight straight nights of *Roots*
and more Black faces than I'd ever seen on TV—
that Alex Haley traced his ancestor
Kunta Kinte from an Annapolis auction block
and the 1767 voyage of the *Lord Ligonier*
to a tribe in the Gambia, West Africa.

I could not pinpoint my ancestral origins.

I did not know how many generations

I would or could go back.

I did not know what I might never know.

But I knew that truth would be hard to come by.

Gorée Island

Decades before my African homecoming,
I had heard of, and written about,
the so-called "slave castles."
Used first for trading gold
and later humans,
dozens of these fortresses dotted
the continent's Gold Coast. Among them,
Cape Coast, Elmina, and our destination: Gorée.

From Dakar, Senegal, we ferry
twenty minutes to Gorée Island,
a carless outpost of volcanic rock
colonized first by Portugal,
later by Holland and France.
On deck, vendors clack kashakas—
percussion instruments made
of two small gourds joined by string.
My son buys some as souvenirs.

Near the dock, La Maison des Esclaves,
the House of Slaves. No castle,
this museum was once a trading post
and a jail, where captive Africans
were held for weeks, months,
until their numbers could fill
a ship's belly or until the next vessel
bound for the Americas arrived.

Narrow slits parse glints of sunlight
into gloomy, thick-walled cells
where men and women, separated,
were crowded and manacled.
If only the walls could bear witness;
confess whether they saw my kin.
Through the Door of No Return,
I peer at the Atlantic Ocean.
Thousands, maybe millions, of Africans
were torn from the Motherland
and herded through that door.

Sun-dappled waves lap at riprap.

If my ancestors were taken from Gorée,
wouldn't I sense their presence?
Wouldn't I hear their cries on the wind,
taste their tears in the salt air,
see their ghosts walking on water?
Absent such signs, I stand silent.
Like a curious child, I quiz Mother Africa.
She offers no answers; only her embrace.

Chesepiooc

AT THE BIG RIVER
CHESAPEAKE BAY

The Algonquians first named me.

The Spaniards called me

Bahía de Santa María,

Bay of Saint Mary.

Explorers mapped my shores

and labyrinth of one hundred fifty tributaries.

Colonists settled my peninsula.

Planters claimed fertile fields,

erected waterfront manors,

and named them: the Anchorage, Fairview, Hope,

the Isthmus, Lombardy, Myrtle Grove,

Peach Blossom, Waverly, and Wye House.

To propel the enterprise, ships

like the *Experiment* brought captive Africans—

a fount of forced labor in perpetuity—

to the ports of Annapolis, Patuxent,

Potomac, and Oxford for auction

or carried them outward to New Orleans—

bound for cotton and sugarcane plantations.
Those same ships docked in the Caribbean,
and carried products like tobacco, wheat,
and wool to trade in England.
Surely as I spill into the Atlantic, the current
of greed swept me into the triangular trade.

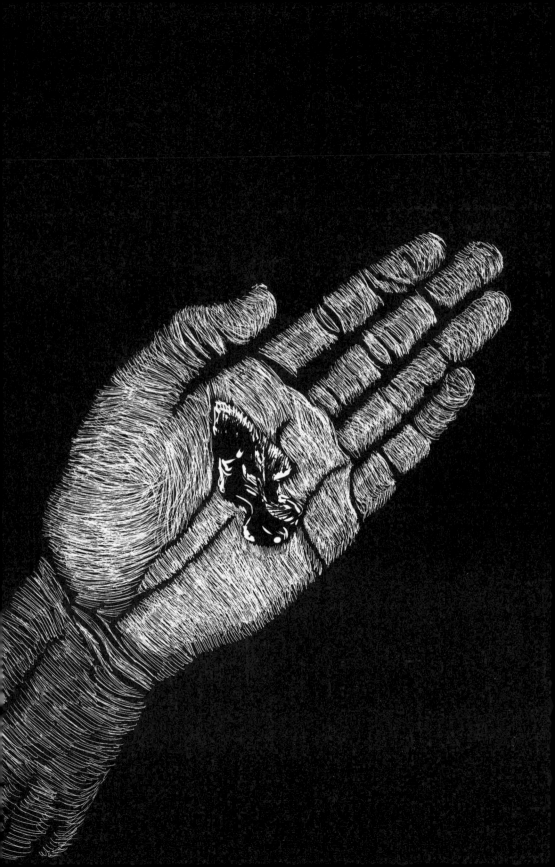

Arrowheads

My farmer friend who has tilled these fields
for decades has found enough arrowheads to fill
a cabinet of curiosities. Relics of tribes
that named rivers: Choptank, Tuckahoe,
Pocomoke, Wicomico, Nanticoke.

These woodland peoples had hunted the forests
and canoed the streams for generations
before trading beaver pelts with white men
for tools, firearms, jewelry, cloth, and "hot water."

The Nations' ancestral lands were carved up
and claimed by European colonists,
and the native population of twenty thousand
was decimated by disease and a twenty-six-year war.

By law, Englishmen could shoot any Indian
who got in their way.

The Native Americans handed down
plant-medicine lore to Black healers.

Centuries later, an archeological dig
at the old Wye House blacksmith shop
found Indigenous pottery and grave goods,
denoting a ceremonial site or a burial ground.

Over time, Native blood mixed with African
and European. The First People are still here—
in spite of the colonial gaze that erased them
and the republic that excluded them from the start.

They still drum Earth's heartbeat
while the rivers sing the Tribes.

The Archeologist

EXCAVATING THE LONG GREEN

Stretching for a clear mile from the Wye River

within view of the overseer's cottage,

the Long Green was the hub

of the plantation known as Wye House.

A village of blacksmiths, carpenters, cobblers,

cooks, coopers, farmhands, gardeners,

grain grinders, sailors, sawyers,

boatbuilders, wheelwrights, and their kin.

And before the colonizers arrived,

sacred ground of Indigenous tribes.

With shovels, trowels, and brushes,

I dust off layers of guilt and shame,

uncovering beads, blown glass, dishes,

teacups, shards of crockery, pins, tools,

cutlery, and a two-headed doctor carving

perhaps signifying an African healer.

I see stones and coins—charms lodged

between masonry to ward off spirits.
Each artifact, a fragment of a larger saga.

Imagine a farmhand—in the few hours
of fading light he has to himself—
carving this button from bone for his beloved.
Imagine her sewing that gift to her only dress.
Between chores, she fiddles with the button,
hoping they are never separated.

The Long Green was a true community,
some families here as far back as they know.
Here, after long hours in the fields or shops,
the enslaved people washed, sewed,
mended, cooked, collected oysters,
and raised their own crops and children.
Here was harsh labor but also love.
Here were shackles but also bonds
sustained by blood and spirits,
sayings, superstitions, and songs.

At nightfall, chants—protesting slavery
and praying for deliverance on earth
or in heaven—rocked the quarter.
Slumber on the heels of singing.
But there was little room or time to rest,
and no beds, just planks or the bare floor
and one coarse blanket per adult.
Young and old, male and female,
married and single all slept together.
Here by the Wye River, how could they not
have dreamed of sailing to freedom?

Wye House
SEAT OF THE LLOYD FAMILY,
LANDED GENTRY

I am the jewel in the Lloyds' crown,

the flagship of the family's vast holdings.

A family whose Puritan patriarch,

Edward Lloyd, arrived in America around 1645

from the British Isles and settled first

in the Virginia colony before migrating

to the Maryland colony where Charles Calvert,

the third Lord Baltimore, granted him land.

Future generations of Lloyds built on

their inheritance, married their fortunes

with other elite families, and grew rich on trade

a century before the Revolution.

No mere manor, I am an agricultural factory.

Turning my gears, hundreds of Black hands,

building barns, minding stables,

stocking storehouses with grains,

and tending tobacco houses.

In the service of the Lloyd family,

kitchens, washhouses, smokehouses,

dairies, summerhouses, greenhouses,

henhouses, turkey houses, and pigeon houses.

To delight the Lloyds and their guests,

bushes, flowers, a deer park, a racetrack, arbors

among shade trees, and an orangerie.

I take my name from the seven-part,

white wooden riverfront mansion

with three wings, a columned portico,

and a circular drive that once saw

less traffic than my Wye River waterfront,

which empties into the Chesapeake Bay.

Not far from the Great House,

generations rest in the family cemetery.

I am proof of the wealth

that America's founding families could amass

by enslaving laborers and marrying money.

Vain without apology, I collect mirrors.

But I cannot face history's reflection.

I witnessed more cruelty than I care to recall.

The sin of slavery haunts my every hall.

Offspring Follows Belly

Hear ye!

A 1662 Virginia legal doctrine declared

that offspring follows the belly,

meaning children born to enslaved mothers

were themselves enslaved—from day one.

This rule applied even when the father

was white or a free Black man.

Other British colonies followed suit.

Thus, enslaved mothers passed down

to their children not only family traits,

but also hereditary life sentences.

Their sole birthright was breath.

When I first see the inventory of property

on the Lloyds' 1781 ledger, I notice four things.

One: My earliest known ancestor, Isaac Copper,

then twenty-one, is the first entry on the page.

Two: Some enslaved people, including Isaac

and his relatives, have surnames.

Three: Names of children of female house servants

are preceded by their mother's first name,

the possessive case denoting maternity—

Alice's Jack, Peg Shaw's Charlotte, Violet's Luce.

Four: The penmanship; the ink, a river

of proof that I have followed to the source.

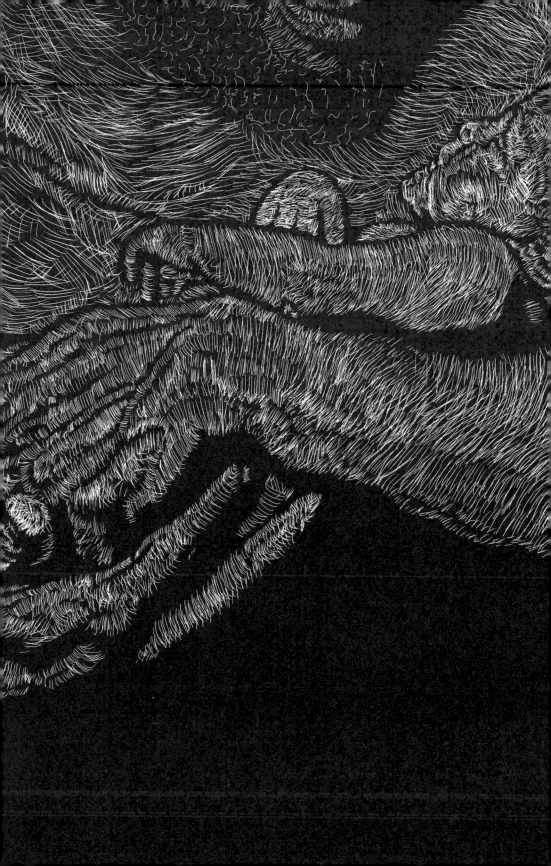

Ages of the Enslaved

ACCORDING TO THE LLOYDS' LEDGERS

At what age is hope born?

Child at one week old

Infant at ½ year

Stout—not good inclined at 11

Promising at 12

Lame in the hip at 12

Small & weakly at 13

Sold at 17

First rate will br[eed] at 17

Common hand at 18

A good hand at 23

When does resistance first rise up?

Indifferent at 25

Stout but bad inclined at 27

An idiot at 28

A bad fellow at 33

Infirm hand at 36

Lame infirm at 39

Lame ankle at 41

Has fits rarely works at 44

Lost a finger at 47

Good of his age at 48

When do dreams wither?

Nearly done at 50

Worth but little at 57

Blind at 60

Unable to work at 62

Past labor at 71

My Lord, how did my kin get over?

What the Lloyds' Ledger Reveals
(1770–1834)

In swirling penmanship: names, ages,

occupations, infirmities, and quality—

ranging from one to four with notes

such as *blind, cripple, past work*, or *good for nothing*—

listed alongside horses, cows, pigs,

bushels of corn, barrels of tobacco,

expenditures on superior sugar, cinnamon,

bisque roses, silver buckles, a gilded mirror,

four dozen pairs of ladies' gloves,

twenty pounds of perfumed hair powder,

sky-blue cloth for six servants' coats,

yellow cloth for breeches and waistcoats,

and a phaeton by London's best carriage maker,

complete with a harness for four.

A fortune built on the backs of enslaved people.

I call their names:

Abram Alice Amey Arianna Antiqua Jemmy

Baker Barnett Beck Benjamin Bett
Big Jacob Blind Sam Cate Charity Charles
Charlotte Cooper Cow
Cuffee Daniel Daphne David Dick and Doll

I call their names:
Ealey Easther Elena Eliza Ennals Esau
Ezekiel Fanny Frances Frank
George Green Harriot Hennyetta
Henry Hester Ann House Jack

And, over generations, the name Isaac—
from 1769, for a child, through 1834,
when a later Isaac with the surname Copper
appears as a house servant—
in the British namesake tradition.

I call their names:
Jake James Jenny Jim John
John Henry Johnson and Joice.
Judith July Anna Jupiter Kitt Laff-ta Little Jacob
Long Jim Lucy Lyddia Mable Marena

Margaret Maria Mary Anna Matt
Merena Milly Molly Nan Nancy
Natt Nedd Nelly Nero Negro Jack
Nurse Henny Old Sam
Old Sarah Old Sue Patience and Peg

I call their names:
Perry Peter Phillis Polly Polodore Prissy
Rachel Richard Rose Sailor Black Harry
Sailor Matt Sailor Ned Sailor Yellow Harry
Sailor Stephen Sall Sally Ann Sam
Sharlotte Sibby Smith Bob Smith Matt Solomon
South River Tom Suckey Tom Virginia Harry
Walter Washington Watt Wesley Will
and Yellow Harry and Yellow Mary

Every last one, property of the Lloyds,
the state's preeminent enslavers.
Every last one, with a mind of their own
and a story that ain't yet been told.

In Search of Stories

In 1860, four million souls were enslaved,
a fraction of the countless captives
brought here and the children born
in bondage since the first kidnapped Africans
arrived in the British North American colonies.
Black voices marginalized, muted, or muzzled.
Black memories taken to the grave
and, over time, forgotten.

There are few documented first-person accounts
of slavery beyond the nineteenth-century narratives
and the reminiscences of aging freedmen
recorded during the Great Depression.
Born in 1872, seven years after freedom,
one generation removed from slavery,
my great-grandpa James Henry Moaney,
never told me that his father, Phillip—
whose portrait overlooked the parlor—
had been enslaved. Grandpa Moaney

did not speak of his father-in-law,
Isaac Copper who fought in the Civil War
after being enslaved at Wye House.
These omissions can be forgiven: I was just
nine years old when Grandpa Moaney died.
Who knows whether Isaac and Phillip shared
their recollections of slavery. Was forgetting
less painful than remembering?
Just as my great-grandfather went blind
and passed on without bearing witness,
the window to my heritage was shuttered.
How could I not let sun in and stories out?

The Choice
SARAH COVINGTON LLOYD (1683–1755)
WIFE OF EDWARD LLOYD II

My father first made a name for himself
stealing cheese. Once an indentured servant
he went on to own five plantations:
Covington's Vineyard, Comfort, and Chance,
and Collin's Adventure and Snow Hill.

Though Quakers, we owned Black people
and willed them to our sons and daughters.
To my sister Priscilla, two, and to my son
Philemon, one girl. We passed down wealth
in three ways: land, silver, and the enslaved.

I first met Major General Edward Lloyd II
at the Great Meeting House at Green Haven.
Anglican. Edward later said he and his brother
Philemon had vied for me as if for a trophy
from the hunt. Edward won.
As his wife, I am the mistress of Wye House—

and to hundreds we hold in bondage.

I strive to treat them fairly but firmly.

I hear some Quakers now condemn slavery.

It offends the Golden Rule, they warn.

My husband's and father's faiths collide.

I dare not challenge either.

Dear Lord.

Dear Lord.

I can only question

my own

soul.

The Lloyds' Lineage

I. EDWARD LLOYD III (1711–1770)

I descend from a long line of Lloyds—
elder sons, mostly Edwards, save one Philemon.
Born at Wye House, I inherit nineteen hundred acres
of land at age eight when my father dies
and another fifteen hundred from my older brother
Philemon, and nine thousand acres from my father's
half brother Robert Bennett.
Blessed with land and political connections,
I serve in the lower and upper houses
of the assemblies, on the governor's council,
and in three revenue posts for the Lords Baltimore,
proprietors of the Maryland colony.
As a merchant, I partner with my brother
and brother-in-law in shipping and trading
tobacco, wheat, and meat to England,
the West Indies, and New England.
In nearby Queen Anne's County,

I operate grist and fulling mills.
During the French and Indian War,
an imperial struggle over territory,
I worry less about reported scalpings
than about the French corrupting
enslaved people with promises of freedom.
My property survives the conflict intact.
When I take my last breath,
I will have expanded my family's holdings
to forty-three thousand acres, securing our place
as the Eastern Shore's wealthiest planters.

II. EDWARD LLOYD IV (1744–1796)

Well-bred and well-read, I own
a private library of more than one thousand volumes.
But rather than spending the Revolution
reading books, I place the public good
above personal gain. I betray my oath
as delegate to the colonial General Assembly
and sign articles justifying resistance.
Hated by Loyalists and hailed by Rebels,
I earn the moniker "The Patriot."

On March 13, 1781, the British plunder

my plantation, taking money, jewels,

twenty-one pounds of silver, and eight Blacks.

After Independence, while I am in Annapolis

at the state legislature, enslaved Blacks

build a new house in the Palladian style—

a grand home complete with a portico.

By 1783, I own 260 Blacks, 147 horses,

799 sheep, 571 horned cattle, 1 schooner,

500 ounces of silver plate, and 72 tracts of land

totaling more than 118,000 acres.

Those I enslave average 35 barrels

of corn and 85 bushels

of wheat apiece, making my farms

among the most profitable in the region.

III. COLONEL EDWARD LLOYD V
OLD MASTER OF WYE HOUSE (1779–1834)

From Wye House, I influence affairs of state,

dine at a mahogany table that seats twenty,

and run the family's Eastern Shore farms:

Wye Town, New Quarter, Timber Neck,

Four Hundred Acres, Presqu'Isle, and Blissland.
Hundreds of Black hands tend wheat, corn,
and tobacco and till my fields into fortune.
Besides farmhands: gardeners, blacksmiths,
wheelwrights, schooners, coopers, carpenters,
sawyers, sailors, sloops, shoemakers, and weavers.
And in the grand manor, house servants.
The boy called Frederick amuses my son
Daniel and waits outside the schoolroom
window while the tutor instructs my children.

I mean for Blacks to tremble when I speak.
One day, I meet a Black man on the road
and ask how his owner treats him.
Colonel Lloyd is a cruel master, he confides,
not knowing who I am. I do not let on.
Soon after, I sell him in chains to a Georgia trader.
Down South, he won't have time to sully my name.

I serve as a state senator and delegate,
Maryland's thirteenth governor and a U.S. senator.
At leisure, I indulge in books, card games,

lawn bowling, billiards, and duck hunting.
I breed the Chesapeake Bay Retriever.
Why should slavery tarnish my legacy?

IV. EDWARD LLOYD VI (1798–1861)

Unlike my father, I am foremost a farmer.
When tobacco profits fall, I turn the fields
into grain. Twenty-one farms across nine thousand acres
rank me the state's leading wheat grower
and cattleman. I own 468 Blacks—
worth more than twenty-eight thousand dollars—too many
to personally account for. My eyes, the overseers,
wield the lash and report runaways.

Noah, 26 years old, 5 feet 10 or 11 inches high, stout
and black, has very full ill-shaped feet and is clumsy
Jenny, 22 years old, chestnut colour, middling size
and a well-shaped woman.
$100 for delivery of the man, $50 for the woman.

I cannot afford to lose a single soul.
With declining profits from grain crops

and a growing population of the enslaved,
my family lacks the funds to run
a sprawling agricultural enterprise.
To reverse our fortunes, I look south
to Mississippi, where cotton is fast
becoming king, and Louisiana, where
sugarcane is "white gold."
Scouting opportunity, I travel south
and give those whom I enslave a chance
to go with me; a reward for good behavior.
When no one takes me up on the offer,
I make relocation a punishment instead.
Left behind to manage Wye House,
my wife, Alicia, writes that she cannot run
the plantation on a mere fifty dollars a month.
For quick cash, I sell some of the enslaved
who traveled with me. All told,
I ship dozens of Black people south.

V. EDWARD LLOYD VII (1825–1907)

My parents groomed me for Princeton,
but, favoring farming over philosophizing,

I follow in my father's footsteps instead.

I settle at Presqu'Isle, my uncle's former plantation.

When the Mexican-American War breaks out,

I form a company made up of my neighbors.

Though a captain, I do not see battle on the border.

Like my forefathers, I enter politics,

serving as a state delegate and senator.

My father leaves Wye House and other Lloyd farms

to me, making me the leading farmer

in Talbot County. His will orders the sale

of farms in Allegany County, Maryland,

and Madison County, Mississippi.

I have also inherited debt and charges—

sisters and in-laws for whom to provide.

When I take over the plantation in 1861,

my eldest son and namesake is just four,

Abraham Lincoln is in the White House

and the War between the States has begun.

With about eighty-seven thousand enslaved,

Maryland straddles North and South

and does not secede from the Union.

I have plans to manumit
all my enslaved laborers in my will.
Emancipation beats me to it.

In 1881, Frederick Douglass returns to Wye House,
arriving by boat from nearby St. Michaels.
There, he makes peace with Thomas Covey,
a notorious slave breaker whose plantation
was named Mount Misery.
Years earlier, after repeated beatings at Covey's hand,
then sixteen-year-old Douglass landed
a punch that knocked his master down.
On our porch, Douglass sips drinks
with my son. I am conveniently unavailable.
Days later, the Chesapeake Bay Yacht Club
requests my resignation for entertaining
a Black man at my home.

Between Rivers

We were swimmers.

Children growing up on the coast
of West Africa could swim by age six.
After one shipwreck, a captive African
swam sixty miles to shore.
At events on or beside American waters,
enslaved people served as lifeguards
in case white landlubbers needed saving.

We were swimmers:
enslaved fishermen, pearl divers,
and deep-sea treasure hunters.
For sport, white spectators wagered
on matchups between us.

We were swimmers
until it dawned on the enslavers
that we might escape by water,
making our trail undetectable
or, even worse, causing loss due to drowning.
Soon, both swimming and giving lessons
were banned until the skill and know-how
was almost lost to onetime mermen.
In place of our natural buoyancy,
enslavers instilled terror, punishing
disobedience with public water torture
and conjuring tales of sea monsters.

Surely, Talbot County, Maryland's
six hundred miles of tidal shoreline,
taunted Black souls who dreaded
the very rivers that offered deliverance.

We were swimmers, baptized in creeks;
the currents, a barrier and a blessing.
If blood is thicker than water,
then our faith is deeper than fear.

Frederick Douglass
AN EDUCATION

Once you learn to read you will be forever free.
—FREDERICK DOUGLASS

Growing up in Maryland, I knew
Frederick Douglass first as the topic
of dinner table talk between my parents.
They referred not to Douglass, the abolitionist
and statesman who had crossed paths
with my enslaved ancestors as a child,
but to the institution that was once
the only high school for Black Baltimoreans.

My father attended Douglass,
where he played trumpet and football.
Later—after service in World War II
and a college degree on the G.I. Bill—
he worked at Douglass for almost three decades,
chairing the Industrial Arts department
and teaching printing. At my mother's urging,

Daddy used my early poems as typesetting exercises
for his students. They learned to run the letterpress
and I learned that my words could endure.
I did not know then that Douglass himself
had been a printer or a beacon of genius.

A training ground for musicians
like Cab Calloway, onetime headliner
at New York's famed Cotton Club,
Douglass was known for its concert choir,
which performed African American spirituals
a cappella and made Handel's *Messiah*—
climaxing with the "Hallelujah Chorus"—
an annual holiday tradition.
Though I went to a newer school,
I took two classes at Douglass—
if swimming and driver's education count.
Douglass was where I mastered land and water
and first felt the freeing power
of swimming a lap or of steering a car.
Each feat, a rite of passage.
From the deck of the Olympic-size pool,
the ever-patient Coach Cragway succeeded
where others had failed—in teaching me to swim.
Douglass was where I conquered fear
at age twelve and dove into the deep end.
Hallelujah! Hallelujah! Hallelujah!

PORTRAIT OF

Frederick Douglass

(1818–1895, BORN FREDERICK
AUGUSTUS WASHINGTON
BAILEY)

I was the most photographed American
of the nineteenth century.

See me as a young man.

Beneath a beaver-trimmed Cossack hat.

As the white-maned Lion of Anacostia.

Onstage at Tuskegee Institute, a college for freedmen.

Among the directors of the Alpha Life Insurance Company.

With my grandson Joseph as he plays the violin.

At my desk—back to the camera.

I know the power of an image.

Now, Talbot County's most famous son,

I was, in my day, a ship caulker, abolitionist,

orator, and publisher of the *North Star* newspaper.

After the Civil War, a public servant who rose

to become minister of the Republic of Haiti.
But long before becoming a statesman,
I was Frederick Augustus Washington Bailey.
I was enslaved. But I didn't know it at first.

I began my days in my grandmother's cabin
on Captain Anthony's Holmes Hill
    Farm.
My mother, hired out to another
    plantation.
I was about six when my grandmother
    took me
to Wye House. Hours later, a child squealed
that my grandmother had gone.
She had left me there; had lied.
Suddenly, I realized I had been enslaved.
The pear that I was chewing soured in my mouth;
I threw the ripe fruit to the ground.

Captain Anthony supervised Wye House.
I lived with him and slept in a closet.
He was my first master and, I later learned,
my father.

My Bondage
and My Freedom

BY FREDERICK DOUGLASS

Among other slave notabilities, I found here one called by everybody, white and colored, "Uncle" Isaac Copper. It was seldom that a slave, however venerable, was honored with a surname. . . . But once in a while, even in a slave state, a negro had a surname fastened to him by common consent. This was the case with "Uncle" Isaac Copper. When the "Uncle" was dropped, he was called Doctor Copper. He was both our Doctor of Medicine and our Doctor of Divinity. Where he took his degree I am unable to say, but he was too well established in his profession to permit question as to his native skill, or attainments. One qualification he certainly had. He was a confirmed cripple, wholly unable to work, and was worth nothing for sale in the market. Though lame, he was no sluggard. He made his crutches do him good service, and was always on the alert looking up the sick, and such as were supposed to need his aid and counsel. His remedial prescriptions embraced four articles. For diseases of the body, Epsom salts and castor oil;

for those of the soul, the "Lord's Prayer," and a few stout hickory switches.

I was early sent to Doctor Isaac Copper, with twenty or thirty other children, to learn the "Lord's Prayer." The old man was seated on a huge three-legged oaken stool, armed with several large hickory switches, and from the point where he sat, lame as he was, he could reach every boy in the room. After standing awhile to learn what was expected of us, he commanded us to kneel down. This done, he told us to say everything he said. "Our Father"—this we repeated after him with promptness and uniformity—"who art in Heaven," was less promptly and uniformly repeated, and the old gentleman paused in the prayer to give us a short lecture, and to use his switches on our backs.

Everybody in the South seemed to want the privilege of whipping somebody else. Uncle Isaac, though a good old man, shared the common passion of his time and country.

the Elder Isaac

I credit Frederick Douglass with leading me
to Doctor and Minister Isaac Copper.
Douglass—enslaved at Wye House
for two years in the 1820s—later wrote
of that time, that place, and an Isaac
who disciplined children with a hickory stick.
I could not believe that I was seeing
that family name in print. I gushed with pride
over this encounter between my ancestor
and the famed abolitionist and statesman.
My blood ran cold, though, when Douglass
described the corporal punishment
meted out during the minister's instruction;
his impression on Douglass dubious at best.

This much I knew: Douglass's Doctor Copper,
so advanced in years that he leaned on a cane,

could not have been my great-great-grandfather

who fought for the Union during the Civil War.

The younger Isaac probably descended from the elder.

And Doctor/Minister Isaac Copper was my forebear

even if the relationship was not yet crystal clear.

Let down, I took my time claiming him as kin.

I could only guess how many generations

separated the two Isaacs and what ties bound.

Part of me was not ready to know.

Five years passed before I pursued the lead.

The questions would not let me rest.

Isaac Copper

(BORN C. 1760 OR 1763)

How did you come to be owned by the Lloyds?
Were you kidnapped near the coast of Africa
or far from it? Did your father, the chief,
send warriors to find you? Were you herded
onto a slave ship while still in your mother's womb?
The *Favourite Polly* from Ghana's Cape Coast Castle?

Had you made the Middle Passage as a tot
or were you old enough never to forget
the faces of the dead and dying Africans
thrown overboard—almost one in four?
On that dreadful voyage, were you lain
on your back with other captives
in the ship's hold or spooned on your side
among many tribes?
Were you taken first to the West Indies
on the *Liberty* to be broken in

and held in a barracoon
until greased with palm oil for auction?

Were you on a later ship, the *Patience*, perhaps,
which landed in Oxford in 1766, the only
slave-trading port on Maryland's Eastern Shore?
Were you the one who arrived in 1762
from Monserrat on the *Charming Anne*?
Who were your gods then?
And what was your given name?
Were you Igbo? Ashanti?

Or did you come along after enslavers
figured that it was cheaper to buy females
and produce babies born into slavery?
Could Poll have been your mother
and Matt or House Jacob your father?
Were John, Matt, and Jacob your brothers
and Priss, Poll, Marena, and Suckey your sisters—
namesakes for your own offspring with Nan?
And how did you come to have a surname?

Does "Copper" denote African adornments,
or the patina of your burnished skin?

Were your parents willed to Edward
by his half brother, Richard Bennett III—
the wealthiest man in North America?
How many times
had you changed hands by 1770
when your name and age—seven—were
listed in an inventory of the late
Edward III's property and personal effects?

What do you recall? The bosom of family,
tribal rhythms, African earth underfoot,
the first time you glimpsed a pale face,
the stench aboard ship,
the auctioneer's gavel,
or only the lapping of the Wye River?
Were you born here, Isaac?
Is Wye House all you know?

Isaac Copper
THE DOCTOR'S CURES

Epsom salts work wonders but are no cure-all.
When one of us is too sick to work,
the master prescribes a teaspoon of tonic:
quinine for muscle cramps and malaria,
castor oil to clean the system of impurities,
and spirit of turpentine for toothache
and bronchitis.

But folks prefer that I treat them.

They put their faith in my pharmacy.

In the woods, I collect herbs, roots, and bark

to prepare balms, poultices, and teas.

Boneset from the edge of the swamp

and mustard plaster for the croup;

sage for sore throats and colicky babies;

spearmint and peppermint for stomachache;

peach tree leaves to expel worms;

horehound for coughs and colds;

pennyroyal for fever; chestnut leaf for asthma;

sassafras and mayapple to cleanse the blood;

red pepper and jimsonweed for joint pain;

comfrey for sprains and fractures;

and snakeroot as an antidote for snakebites.

In the wrong hands, plants can be poison,

but in righteous hands, strong medicine.

I lay my hands on the sick and pray.

Colonel Lloyd

GOUT, THE "RICH MAN'S ARTHRITIS"

I delight in rich foods and imported spirits,
but would not wish this "disease of kings"
on my worst foe. After retiring, I sleep
soundly until pain seizes my calf, ankle,
heel, or big toe as if my joints are dislocated.
Chills, shivering, and fever overtake me
as the pain intensifies; made worse
by the weight of my nightshirt
and floorboards shaking underfoot.

Is God punishing me? I moan to Isaac
as he mixes my medicine, using
my doctor's recipe: seedless raisins,
rhubarb, coriander, cochineal, fennel seed,
saffron, sumac, and licorice in brandy.
For ten days, I sip the concoction.
When the pain is acute, I wonder
how much longer I can serve as a senator.
On bad days, I cannot mount my horse
and can barely climb into a carriage.

Isaac Copper
WHY I AM CALLED DOCTOR
OR MINISTER

When you are among the few
who can remember the Motherland
or who heard firsthand accounts of it,
you must keep watering those roots.

When you are the only one who knows
for sure that he descends from African royalty,
you must take the lead in teaching others,
even if prayer is the only education allowed the enslaved.

When you are the keeper of stories, cures, and rituals,
you must tell your children their heritage.
You must summon the power of shamans
and healers and the ancient wisdom of the elders.

When you are past labor, you hold a two-faced carving
in one hand and a cane with the other.
You make magic bundles of stones and coins
and poultices from plants in the hothouse.

When you are the only one who knows,
you tell somebody; you show someone.
You remember for those who might forget.
You pass it down.

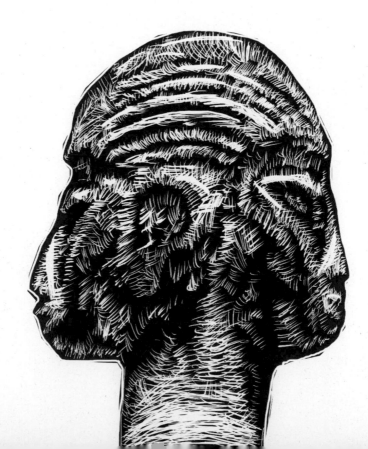

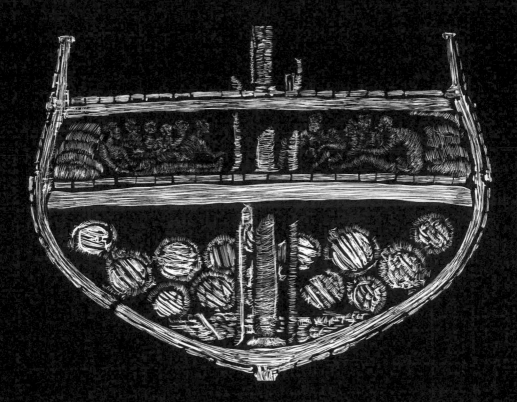

PORT OF OXFORD, MARYLAND COLONY, 1763

*A Tale of the Two Sisters and
the Two Brothers Edward and Richard?*

What is the chance that Isaac was on one

of these vessels: the *Two Sisters*

or the *Edward and Richard*? The latter—

owned by Edward Lloyd IV and named

for his two sons—sailed from St. Kitts,

West Indies, and landed in Oxford in 1767

with eleven enslaved Africans.

The *Two Sisters* reached the same port
four years earlier.
Captain Jeremiah Banning recorded
the voyage of the one-hundred-sixty-ton ship from London
to Guernsey to Senegal and Gorée
en route to the Maryland colony.
With seven guns and a twenty-man crew
that would fight pirates off the Barbary Coast
and the shoals, surf, and currents at the mouth
of the Senegal, the *Two Sisters* reached
Africa on June 12, cannons roaring a salute.

The King of Senegal greeted the guests.
Clad in a plaid caftan, checked pants, and red slippers,
he offered hospitality while asking about
the cargo and the Crown. On Gorée Island,
with the local governor, Banning traded
passage to Senegal, a Guernsey cow,
his coat and brass ship's clock
for ten captive Africans.
In that lot: Ishinnee and her three children—
Lucy, Juba, and Scipio. The *Two Sisters*

departed Gorée with British officers
and African royalty aboard.

In Senegal, a woman
from a royal family glimpsed
her brother among the captives.
For his release, she paid five gold bars
and two men whom she herself enslaved.
That very evening, three remaining captives
escaped on the stern boat. Ship's crew
in pursuit, one man was recaptured and two
jumped overboard, choosing hungry sharks
over chains. The gold bars also went missing.
The *Two Sisters* left Africa July 14 and arrived
in Oxford on August 29. Customs records
attest to cargo of five Africans and a ton of sassafras.

I can't help but wonder whether royal blood
coursed through those five who survived
the Middle Passage, princes or princesses
whom no one had spoken for or saved.
Is either ship a lifeline in this uncharted sea?

Captain Richard Bruff

(1705–1760)

From a family of innkeepers and silversmiths,

remembered as a cabinetmaker

and as a reader during Sunday service,

Richard Bruff was first a merchant and a mariner,

who plied the Bay and the Atlantic

with his quadrant, hanging compass, spyglass,

nocturnal, and surveying equipment.

That is how I came to know him.

A sloop built in Maryland in 1748

and registering forty tons,

I sail from the port of Oxford in 1752,

pregnant with the promise of profit,

my belly full of cargo. With wind

and money in my sails, I convey

sought-after goods from port to port

to benefit my owner, planters,

merchants, insurers, and banks.

With Richard Bruff as captain,
I sail fourteen hundred nautical miles
south to Antigua, West Indies—
a twelve-mile-wide sugar island
where Blacks outnumber whites eight to one.

Only sixteen years earlier, the court there
ordered public executions after a rumored plot
by Blacks to set off an explosion at a ball
and kill all whites on the island.
Led largely by artisans, Creoles,
and servants whom enslavers
never guessed might have cause to rebel,
the plan was hatched by Kwaku—
a Ghanian given the slave name "Court"
and memorialized as Prince Klaas.

As punishment for the alleged conspiracy,
eighty-eight Black people were killed:
six hanged in chains and starved to death,
seventy-seven burned at the stake,
and five tortured through bone-crushing
crucifixion on the breaking wheel.

Brutal sentences aimed to squash any notions
of revolt and to protect white lives and livelihoods.

As I anchor in the harbor,
more than one hundred fifty windmills
greet me at sugarcane plantations.
The stone windmills turn and turn
as enslaved Black boilers and distillers
work twenty-four-hour days
in the sweltering mill during harvest.

Moored at the dock, I leave Antigua
without ever tasting the confection
that has driven men to enslave others.
I am no vessel for sweet memories.
With Captain Bruff and six crew,
and thirty-eight Black souls in my hold,
I depart Antigua. On October 21, 1752,
we dock in Oxford, Maryland.
I bore thirty-seven Blacks into bondage
in the British colonies, having lost but one
Black captive en route from Antigua.
Yet my belly is full of regret.

Though owned by James Dickenson,

I share the Old Testament name

Rachel with Captain Bruff's mother and sister—

after the woman who married Jacob

and gave birth to Benjamin and Joseph,

forebears of two of the Twelve Tribes of Israel.

Captain Bruff resurrected these names

for the two sons—Ben and Jacob—

he had by Rose, an enslaved teenager.

I had no more say in carrying my cargo

than Rose did in bearing those children.

Captain Richard Bruff's
BRIEF MARITIME CAREER

I can hardly imagine the Lloyds and Bruffs
being unacquainted, given the nearness
of their properties. The Bruffs' island
was just over a mile by boat and foot
from Wye House, and their plantation
in the now-lost town of Doncaster
was less than two miles away on horseback.
The two families
even had business dealings, said isle
being sold in 1720 to Edward Lloyd II's
half brother, Richard Bennett III,
who graciously renamed it Bruff's Island.

Isn't it possible that Edward Lloyd II
placed an order for a few dozen
African captives to work tobacco
when he heard that Captain Richard Bruff,
whom he'd known almost his whole life,

was sailing for Antigua? Wasn't that
how gentlemen conducted business?
The captain might even have delivered
the cargo directly to the Wye House dock.
Could my ancestors Poll, Jacob, and Matt
have been among those thirty-seven?
I may never know.

Census: Terminus

Between 1695 and 1773,
seventy-eight voyages landed
more than thirty-eight hundred
enslaved African descendants in Annapolis.
The most famous among them, Kunta Kinte—
the African ancestor of *Roots* author Alex Haley—
is remembered with a bronze plaque at the city dock.
Another three hundred ninety enslaved Blacks
landed in Oxford between 1696 and 1772.
Absent manifests or auction receipts
with Anglicized names, I can only speculate
about which ships my kin came over on,
the years that they arrived in Maryland,
and the places that their journeys began.
I gain no satisfaction from knowing
that old Doctor Isaac Copper,
whose name I first saw on a 1781 ledger
and whom young Frederick Douglass met,
was already at Wye House by 1769.
Isaac was only six or nine years old then.

Young Isaac
(1770)

Before the Boston Tea Party protested
taxation without representation,
I was training to serve exotic teas
in porcelain cups and saucers.

Before the First Continental Congress
convened and Patrick Henry proclaimed,
"Give me liberty or give me death!"
my childhood had come to an end.

Before Paul Revere warned of British invasion
and Thomas Jefferson drafted
the Declaration of Independence,
my freedom was already hostage.

Before Crispus Attucks, a free Black man,
fell at the Boston Massacre, becoming
the first fatality of the American Revolution,
I had resisted the urge to rebel, to run.

Before General George Washington
crossed the Delaware River, I sat
on the banks of the Wye, wondering:
How far to Africa?

Before the Patriots defeated the Redcoats
to free the new republic from the Crown,
my royal ties were robbed from me.
But Africa drummed in my heart.

Nan
(AGE SEVEN, 1770)

The Great House would be a lonely place

were it not for Isaac working alongside me.

There is no time for play, but we do

exchange glances sometimes and share

smiles while we learn our appointed tasks.

We may let out a giggle when Miss Sarah,

the housekeeper, is not within earshot.

We make games of our chores.

Who can climb the stairs the fastest?

Who can make the silliest faces

in the mansion's many mirrors?

Sad-eyed, we compare our lot

to that of the lucky Lloyd children.

As they do lessons or play with toys,

we long for their charmed lives.

Amidst our unending errands

against this lavish backdrop,

we wonder what our future holds.
The only thing greater than this house
is my hope to someday leave it.

1770: An Uncertain Time

1770. The year of the Boston Massacre,
that Marie Antoinette arrived at Versailles,
that poet Phillis Wheatley became
the first African and only the second woman
to be published in the Americas,
that Edward Lloyd III's will was read,
which inventoried Isaac and Nan
along with other worldly goods.
If ever there was praying in the Long Green,
the quarter, it was at that moment.
Not grief-struck but terror-plagued,
enslaved residents knew that their late master's
mismanaged estate was to be split in three
equal lots among his eldest son,
son-in-law, and unmarried daughter.
Do the math. One hundred seventy-four
Black folks could be divided from kin,
subtracted from one plantation,
and added to another someplace else.
The Lloyds strove to keep families
of farm laborers intact to deter escape.

Still, uncertainty gripped the Long Green.

Work slowed and crop yields plummeted.

Labor as leverage.

More often torn from their families

than the enslaved at other Lloyd farms,

Blacks at Wye House, Home House,

had even more to fear.

When Edward III's estate was settled,

Edward IV, Henrietta Maria Lloyd,

and General John Cadwallader, husband

of Elizabeth Lloyd, each inherited livestock,

silver, and furniture worth 1,367 pounds

and drew lots for a labor force valued

at 2,400 pounds. The will did grant

enslaved house servants the privilege

of objecting to their allotment in favor

of another heir. For the exchange,

the chosen master had to pay the spurned

heir *the value of the unwilling servant.*

Young Isaac and Nan were both in lot three,

which went to Edward Lloyd IV.

They would remain at Wye House.

Together.

Nanny / Nancy / Nan Copper,
(BORN C. 1763, HOUSE SERVANT)

My name is also my duty.

Nanny to Colonel Lloyd's children.

I was a child myself the first time

I held a little Lloyd in my arms.

Isaac and I have our own babies,

but I still tend the Lloyd children

in the Great House. They cry after me

as if I gave birth to them

and suck milk from my breasts

instead of their mama's.

If the little missy wants to play horsey,

I kneel on all fours and ride her on my back.

I bathe, clothe, and feed the Lloyd children

while my children eat from troughs

in the quarter until they're old enough to work.

I pray that Colonel Lloyd won't sell them.

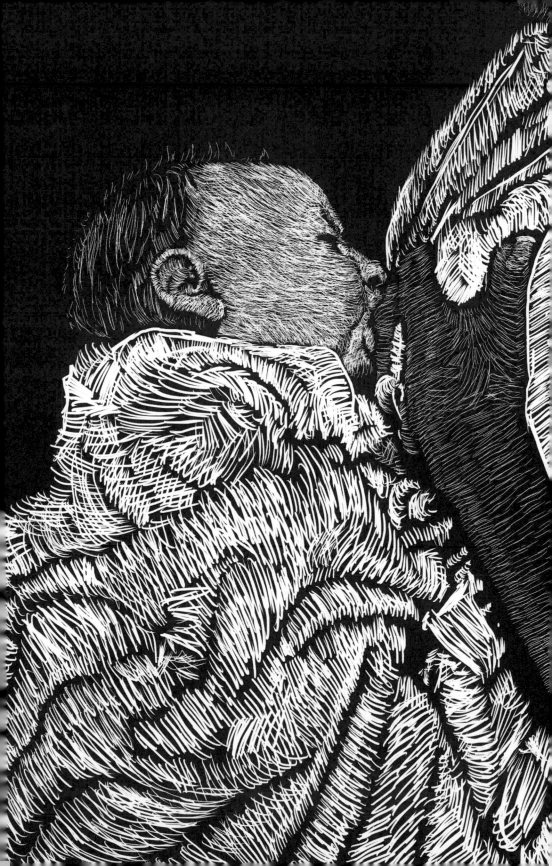

Isaac Copper

(BORN C. 1760 OR 1763,
HOUSE SERVANT)

I came up with Peter, Lucy, Henny, Sall,
Katy, Daphne, Sue, and Nan.
In the Great House, Charity, Old Suckey, Peg Shaw,
Nurse Henny, and Barnett taught us
to wait on the Lloyds and their guests.

We learned early to mind the children,
gather wood, feed chickens, clean house,
and shoo flies and mosquitoes. Farmhands
think house servants have it easy.

But in the Great House, there's no escaping
the Lloyds' gaze. Nearness allows
constant supervision. Minor mistakes
provoke harsh words; fair questions,
a slap in the face. Even failure to foresee a need

is cause for a flogging. Within striking distance,

the master can even whip me himself.

The missus's foul mood is my misfortune.

If I flee, they will notice right away.

Nanny and Isaac Copper
OUR CHILDREN

We have eight children:

Sam, born 1787

Prissy, born 1788

Henny, born 1792

Suck/Suckey, born 1792

Polly, born 1794

Marena, born 1796 (house servant)

Isaac, born 1798 (shoemaker/house servant)

Henry, born 1800.

They were all Coppers

born at Wye House,

named for kin who came before—

a tradition that continued

until well after Reconstruction.

Over time, Coppers would connect

by blood or marriage with Johnsons,

Moaneys, Blakes, Roberts, Suttons,

and folks denied surnames or lines
in any ledger and with enslaved people
from various Eastern Shore plantations
owned by Lloyds, Hollydays, Bennetts,
Goldsboroughs, and Tilghmans.
Living in close quarters, circles
of fathers, mothers, sisters, brothers,
aunts, uncles, in-laws, double
and distant cousins leaned on
one another until kin became
synonymous with community.

Missing Faces

In the entry hall of Wye House hangs
an oil replica of Charles Willson Peale's
1771 portrait, *Family of Edward Lloyd*.
Edward IV, Elizabeth, and daughter Ann
strike a pose befitting prominent planters.

Edward IV, wig powdered, hand on hip,
wears a red velvet, gold-trimmed suit.
Hair bejeweled, his wife, Elizabeth,
in sequined, sky-blue silk and Chantilly lace,
strums a cittern. Toddler Ann,

beside her mother on the bench
in a tucked, Empire-waist frock,
hikes her skirt to reveal its pale pink lining.
A moment captured as a conversation piece.
Elsewhere in the Great House, silhouettes,

etchings and ink drawings imprint privilege
upon successive generations of Lloyds.
Absent are the visages of my ancestors
who dutifully ordered the opulent clutter.
They hanged the Lloyds' framed conceits,

dusted ivory carvings and crystal candelabra,
and polished treasures atop sideboards.
Once the house servants' burden,
the décor endures. But the faces
of my kin have vanished.

Erased.

Daphne Irons

(BORN C. 1750, HOUSE SERVANT)

Ironing is hard, hot work:

silk, cotton, linen, and wool garments

from the Lloyds' mahogany wardrobes.

I push the flat iron to smooth wrinkles

until linens are as crisp as sails

and silks as fluid as the creek.

Draping gathers and folds,

I admire the fabrics' hand.

So much suppler than burlap,

so much softer than tow linen

or the coarse linen of the few garments

allotted annually to my people.

Within months, our outfits are rags.

But that does not strip dignity;

my inner fiber—strong as this here iron.

Sall Makes Terrapin Soup

There are seven kinds of meat on a terrapin
or snapping turtle as some folks call it.
Different parts taste like turkey, fish, pork, or veal.
Maryland waters are full of terrapins—so many
that codes forbid masters from feeding it
to the enslaved more than twice a week
for fear our diet would consist of little else.
Can't count how many turn up in my kitchen.
I figure every terrapin I fix for the Lloyds
is one my people ain't got to stomach.

Chicken Sue

The English Game fowl is for cockfights
that quench Master's bloodthirst
and satisfy his appetite for betting.
When that rooster crows at daybreak,
I am already in the barnyard,
tending fowl: guinea hens from Africa,
domesticated Muscovy ducks,
and dominique and Nankin chickens.
The Lloyds relish game birds, too:
goose, pheasant, turkey, quail,
partridge, pigeon, and even the swan.
Somehow, chickens got left out of the law
against enslaved people raising and selling
livestock, so I can sell birds from the flock
that I keep in the quarter. I don't own house
nor hut, but these chickens are all mine.
I fret when a hen goes missing. But if I clip
their wings, I fear forgetting how to fly.

to work in the Great House kitchen

or to serve the Lloyds and their guests,

Colonel Lloyd had me cook for my people.

To each enslaved person, a monthly ration

of eight pounds of fish or pickled pork,

one bushel of gritty cornmeal, and a pint of salt.

Food more fit for hogs.

Now, instead of plucking feathers from fowl,

instead of picking crab and shucking oysters,

instead of roasting prime rib and venison,
I cure tainted pork and small fish
that should have been thrown back.
Instead of baking bread and pastries,
I fire ashcakes on glowing coals.

With no time to spare from chores,
my people eat where they work—
the field, the barn, the workshops.
Lord knows how we labor so hard
and long with so little food to go on.
I dole out the stingy allotment
as best I can to make it last all month.
I am up in age and hungry myself.

Marena Copper

(BORN 1796, DAUGHTER OF ISAAC AND NANNY COPPER)

My name mirrors the sea on a moonlit night.

But this riverfront plantation is close

as I've come to *Reverie*, the schooner

that buoys my hopes, saves me

from drowning in drudgery.

As captain of that vessel, I have kin

aboard and a starlit route on my palm.

My lifeline joins family and freedom.

Eyeing the port of Liberty, I prepare to dock.

Ma-re-na! Ma-re-na! Ma-re-na!

Loud as any ship's horn,

Missus Lloyd's voice rips me

from this mirage and tugs me

back to bed-changing chores.

This anchor, really a ball and chain;

and the sails, clean sheets billowing.

A house servant like my ma and pa,

I was chosen for my bearing.

My cotton, silk, and wool garments show

that Colonel Lloyd can afford to adorn

his dozen house servants like decor.

We are the picture of his prosperity,

the hands of his hospitality,

the very gesture of his gentility.

Domestic service is no privilege.

By boat and by carriage, summer guests

stream to Wye House, enticed

by bay breezes and a bountiful table.

The house, almost acting as an inn;

its mahogany table draped in fine lace

and set with English crystal, china, and silver.

I polish silverware and pick flowers

for centerpieces while the cooks prepare.

The feast: fruits of the land, sky, and sea,

crops that were raised by the farmhands,

fine wines shipped from across the ocean,

and sugary confections. If I give in
to my sweet tooth, take the tiniest taste,
I could wind up with an iron bit
in my mouth as punishment.
As I clear a course, guests, bellies full, grunt.

Contrast this menu with the meager fare
the master allows us—we who raise, cook,
and serve the food. The leavings; slop.
Enslaved children fan the guests.
Candlelit chatter drags on with toasts
and clinking goblets. A curtain of stars
pleats the sky through the parlor windows.
I yawn, wishing the guests would retire.
I am invisible, yet I cannot disappear.
My folks should have named me Patience.

Marena Copper

MARINER

1829—

my maiden voyage. I sailed

to eternity.

Prissy

HOUSE SERVANT
(BORN 1788, DAUGHTER OF ISAAC
AND NANNY COPPER)

Since I was old enough to reach a table,
I have worked in the Great House with my folks.
Early on, I could set a table and curtsy.
In silk dresses that Colonel Lloyd's daughters
tired of and cast aside as out of fashion,

I admire my reflection in a gilded looking glass.

I am more well versed in etiquette

than some of the guests that I serve.

One dinner guest remarks that my name

comes from the Bible—the New Testament.

Says he'd like to stay with me

like Paul did with Priscilla in Corinth.

Prissy is not short for Priscilla,

I want to say. *Prissy is my whole name.*

As I serve dessert, the man licks his lips,

says he'd like a taste of me. I want to say,

You already have:

I spit in your soup.

Chessie

THE CHESAPEAKE BAY RETRIEVER

Artist and naturalist John James Audubon called
the bay the nation's "greatest resort of waterfowl."
There, I am in my element. I descend from Sailor,
a Newfoundland-like male that Edward Lloyd V
procured in 1807 in exchange for a merino ram.
At Wye House, Sailor mated with other retrievers,
becoming the father of my line. To this day,
I am the only American-bred retriever.

My chocolate-brown, deadgrass, or sedge
coloring blends with the brush as I flush out
game from their roosts. Wings flapping wildly,
the flock alights into the hunter's sight. Bang!
The prey drops, and I dash into the chilled chop
of the bay's northern necks to retrieve it.
My dense, wavy coat of slick, oily fur may stink,
but it is waterproof and withstands the cold.
I will even break ice to bring back waterfowl—
up to three hundred ducks or geese a day.

More complex than the average gundog,
I have a stubborn streak but a loyal heart.
I would never bite hands that feed me.
I guard my owners ferociously and can track,
or sniff out trouble, if pressed into service.
But don't think that I relish running with the packs
of bloodhounds, foxhounds, Scottish staghounds,
bull dogs, or curs that patrollers sic on runaways.
Catching Black people is not my idea of sport.

Daniel Lloyd

(1812–1875), SON OF EDWARD LLOYD V,
SPEAKS OF FREDERICK DOUGLASS

How fortunate am I that Captain Anthony
owned a Black boy named Fred
and that the captain's daughter
Lucretia arranged for Fred to be plucked
from among eighty other Black children
to be the young master's companion?

How blessed is Fred not to work in
   the fields,
and to, instead, be my playmate?
We fish, hunt rabbits, and play games
of my choosing. I protect Fred from the
   big boys.
When my family entertains and guests
descend on Wye, I always bring Fred cake,
and crumbs from conversations.

While I am tutored in the Great House,
Fred waits outside the "school" room window
listening, perhaps to birds, but absorbing
not one morsel of knowledge from my lessons.
I recite alphabets and spell out words
from the hornbook until I am bored.
How lucky is Fred to be unsuited for learning?

If I were older, I would buy him
so we can always be close.

Frederick Douglass
REMEMBERS HIS MOTHER

My first summer at Wye House,
hunger lodged in my belly like a boarder.
I had gotten on Aunt Katy's bad side
and she fed me so poorly that I stole
leathery bacon skin, roasted kernels
of Indian corn—barely enough for a field mouse—
and was ready to fight Nep, the old dog,
for the crumbs and small bones flung
from tablecloths that servants shook.

Just when I thought I'd starve, my mother
showed up with a hug and ginger cake
for me and a warning for Aunt Katy.
My mother had walked twelve miles
to feed me enough love to sustain me.
I fell asleep knowing that I mattered,
that I had a throne in my mother's heart.
The next morning, she was gone.
And I never saw her again.

Minister Isaac Copper
PREACHES TWICE

I preside over two worship services—

one within earshot of the master or overseer,

and the other for my people and my God.

To appease the white men, I preach obedience,

holding to the Ten Commandments

and to prayers that mimic our master's.

Later, by moonlight in the forest,

a secret gathering where the Spirit

has free reign. With an iron pot

turned upside down to sanctify

the ground and muffle sound, true

believers commence singing,

sending up prayers on crescendos,

rounds of sorrow songs. Testimonies

peppered with amens, shouts,

and trembling. Praise shakes

darkness from the night

and ushers in the dawn.

My Lord, what a morning

When the stars began to fall.

Big Jacob, THE GARDENER (C. 1767)
Little Jacob (C. 1768)
Kitt (C. 1744, PERHAPS FEMALE)
Stephen (C. 1749)

The latest advances from the master's books
and the science of Mr. McDermott, a gardener
imported from Scotland, come to fruition—
thanks to enslaved gardeners like us—
in the culinary, ornamental, and medicinal gardens.
We tend the orchard, harvest the fruit,
and work in the greenhouses, too.
The hothouse is a true wonder.

They call it the orangerie. We stoke the furnace
powering the hypocaust that blows heat
under the floor. The orangerie even has
a water pump, and a thermometer to check
the temperature. The hothouse yields
a year-round bouquet of roses, irises,
pond lilies, and hibiscus, and a bounty
of citrus and tropical delights: bananas,

plantains, oranges, lemons, and limes.
Though denied us, lemons are prized
for treating maladies. One man rode
eighteen miles on horseback to fetch
a lemon for his ailing wife.
Is any forbidden fruit more bitter
than the miracle cure right in our midst?

Colonel Lloyd does not allow our people
to set foot in the garden unless ordered.
It is not for our pleasure.
The chief gardener whips
any Black man, woman, or child
who picks so much as a berry.
To snare us if we enter the garden,
Colonel Lloyd has the fence tarred.
Anyone tar-stained is deemed guilty
and punished. No questions asked.

Fruits of Whose Labor?

As I walk through the barren orangerie,
I imagine it when the furnace still functioned,
warming the hothouse to force tropical fruit
to grow farther from the equator than nature
ever intended. Through a wall of windows,
the sun fills the room once lined
with potted lemon, lime, orange, and banana trees.
Unlike my ancestors, also robbed from the tropics,
the exotic fruits cannot endure northern winters.

Adjacent to the expansive hothouse, a room
where the enslaved worker who minded
the furnace may have lived with his family.
The room was none too shabby for a slave quarter,
I am told, by a man who resides in a mansion.
No space is ample, I want to say,
for those being held against their will.
I wonder if my kin worked in the orangerie,
whether they ever once tasted lemon—
to this day, my favorite flavor.

Design for a Plantation Garden

TARRED FENCE TARRED FENCE TARRED FENCE TARRED FENCE TARRED FENCE TARRED FENCE

Culinary

Radishes	Beets	Parsnips	Carrots
Peas	French beans	French beans	Peas
Squash	Tomatoes	Tomatoes	Squash
Artichokes	Onions	Onions	Artichokes
Asparagus	Celery	Celery	Asparagus
Squash	Pumpkin	Pumpkin	Squash
Blueberries	Raspberries	Raspberries	Blueberries
Chard	Broccoli	Broccoli	Chard
Cucumbers	Cantaloupe	Cantaloupe	Cucumbers
Rhubarb	Watermelon	Watermelon	Rhubarb
Potatoes	Potatoes	Potatoes	Potatoes
Cauliflower	Lettuce	Lettuce	Cauliflower

NO NEGROES NO BLACKS NO ENSLAVED NO AFRICANS N

Fruit Orchard

Apple	Apple	Apple	Apple

Medicinal/Herbal

Lavender	Basil	Sage	Thyme
Chives	Mint	Yarrow	Dill
Parsley	Apothecary's rose	Coriander	Oregano
Bee balm	Anise	Caraway	Comfrey
Fennel	Feverfew	Lungwort	Hyssop
Bloodwort	Coriander	Tarragon	Savory

Household

Bedstraw	Madder	Woad	Sweet woodruff
Teasel	Violets	Santonila	Pennyroyal

Floral

Black-eyed Susan	Nasturtium	Sweet William	Creopsis
Hollyhock	Johnny Jump-ups	Peony	Hollyhock

Pear	Pear	Pear	Pear

Henry Copper
(BORN 1800)

The cruelest of all overseers
was rightly named Mister Sevier.
His tongue was most foul.
At young ones, he'd scowl
while whipping their mothers to tears.

Yellow Molly
(AKA MOLLY YELLOW)
SHORT FOR "MULATTO"?

Recipe for yellow dye:
Make a strong decoction
of hickory bark chips. Strain.
Mix in sulphur. Boil cloth
until the color pleases.

Whom does my color please?
Did love die or ever live
on the pallet where I was made?
Who dyed me telltale ocher?
How to explain me or Yellow Harry
(not to be confused with Black Harry)?

My paternity is no mystery;
my only surname, a euphemism:
"child of the plantation," meaning
my mama was enslaved and my pa was white.
Their union was either a sin—
if the white preacher is to be trusted—

or a crime, at least under colonial law:
Marriage between white women
and free Negro or mulatto men is forbidden.
Any white man that shall intermarry
with any Negro or mulatto woman,
such Negro or mulatto shall become a slave
during life, excepting mulattoes
born of white women, who,
for such intermarriage, shall only
become servants for seven years.

I never got to ask my mama about my pa
because she was sold south before I could
string words into a question, before her face
could imprint in my memory.
Folks say that my mistress banished her
and forbade me from darkening the door.
Under the hot sun, I turn russet and blister.

Neither my name nor my complexion
was of my choosing. Yellow brings no favor,
only unwanted advances from white men

who pleasure themselves at my expense.
Once, one of them snuck me a lemon
from the hothouse. As I tasted the tang,
he told me that Molly, in Hebrew,
means bitter. I suppose the name suits me.

Field Hands

Before sunup, the horn summons us
to the fields. Anyone lagging
gets the overseer's hickory stick.

Crops change over time,
but the hard work never ceases.

At first, tobacco, the golden leaf,
twelve hours a day, six days a week,
ten months a year, from February
or March to November or early December.

Tobacco, so prized before the Revolution
that it is used in Maryland as money.

But we Africans are worth more.

When planters shift to grain:
more intense labor, more work
between harvest and planting,
and one more hour of evening chores.

When we come in from the fields,
we husk and shell maize

and sort and tie hands of tobacco.
In the winter, we clear land,
cut firewood, plough the ground,
thresh and clean the grain harvest,
sow oats and hay for the livestock,
and build or repair rail fences.
Only in the worst weather, a day off.
Not even the meanest overseer
wants to supervise in snow or sleet.

Barnett

(BORN 1766, SON OF HOUSE SERVANT
PEG SHAW)

I bet the stables and carriage-houses here
are as grand as any over in Europe.
The Lloyds' three shiny coaches
are cushioned enough for slumber.
Gigs, barouches, sulkies,
and sleighs are stored here too,
along with expensive saddles and harnesses,
and three dozen thoroughbreds,
prized for speed, agility, and spirit.

I work harder than these beasts.
It takes two, me and my son, to groom
horses, clean stables, and drive carriages.
If the horses give Master any problem—
hang their heads low or move too slow—
he complains that the animals
were not sufficiently rubbed or curried,
were kept too warm or cool,

had the wrong food, too little food,

or the wrong amount of moisture.

Young Barney and I get blamed.

Master whips us before he will a horse.

From the stable, we hear hounds

baying in their house nearby.

Even they eat better than my people.

I exercise the horses, rushing like wind

until trees blur and heartbeat

and hoofbeat become one

pounding, resounding rhythm.

If not for family, I would gallop,

gallop far away.

Breeding

I. Elizabeth Tayloe Lloyd (1750–1825)

I am a gentlewoman of exquisite breeding.
Having inherited twenty thousand acres
and three hundred twenty enslaved people,
my father, John Tayloe, built Mount Airy plantation
overlooking the Rappahannock River.
In the Virginia colony, the Tayloe name
is synonymous with horse breeding.
Our stable boasts progeny
of the imported gray mare Medley
whose colts, my father proclaimed,
were the best racers we ever produced.
Along with a hope chest full of linens,
I carried the equestrian tradition
into my marriage to Edward Lloyd IV
of Wye House. At our private track,
Racehorse Point, our pride and joy chase
each other ahead of public races
in Easton, Oxford, Chestertown, or Annapolis.

For me, nothing compares to the surge
of muscle and momentum
thundering down the homestretch,
jockeys jostling, jolting for position.
A winning rider is worth more than
his weight in purses or bragging rights.
Unlike the racehorses that we breed,
a good jockey is rarely put up for auction;
his place in our enterprise, forever secure.
I have an eye on Young Barney.

II. YOUNG BARNEY

Someday, in a silk jacket,
I will ride a horse like Medley
into the record books.
I will win so many purses
that the Lloyds will repay me
with manumission.
One day, I will buy
my own thoroughbred,
a black mare, sixteen hands tall.
I will name him Freedom.

Odds

The rich could afford to wager on any contest:

a billiards game on the second floor of the orangerie,

prized thoroughbreds bolting around Racehorse Point,

or a cockfight, a blood sport if ever there was one.

Enslaved people had nothing to wager, but they knew

that the odds were one to two that if sold,

they would be torn from their parents or spouse.

And, of those sold, one in four would be children.

I wager the threat of sale haunted them each day.

Joseph Copper
FLIES THE COOP, 1809

There is only one Joseph Copper
in the Lloyds' multiyear ledger
and he was born in 1834—too late
to have been the Joseph Copper
whose name entered the public record
as a runaway in 1809. The elder Joseph
for being born into slavery, and the younger
for seeking liberation from shackles.
Undeterred by the likelihood
of a relentless chase or retribution
if returned to slavery, Joseph Copper
chose late spring 1809 to escape.

There is no indication of whether
Joseph was a house servant, field hand,
or an artisan, or of what provoked
his escape that May. Had he decided
with his head or with his heart? Perhaps

he had heard he would be sold south,

had been beaten too many times,

or had made a pact with his beloved

to escape their respective plantations.

Had the abolition of the transatlantic

slave trade made domestic slavery

even more brutal and unbearable?

How long had Joseph Copper plotted

before the waxing gibbous moon

signaled, *Tonight?*

How soon after did the master note

Joseph's absence and place this notice

in the May 23 *Republican Star?*

200 DOLLARS REWARD.

ABSCONDED from the subscriber,

A few days since, negro Joseph Copper—

he is about five feet ten inches high,

with rather small eyes and a very long under lip,

his feet are large, and remarkably full

and round on the inner side of the instep

above the hollow of the foot.

He moves clumsily in his common walk

and has a loud and rather hoarse voice.

The above reward will be given for delivering

him to the subscriber, if taken out of state—

fifty dollars if taken out of the county—

and thirty if taken in the county. EDWD LLOYD.

Once captured, Joseph Copper was sold.

I wish his story had a better ending.

Charles Copper

(BORN 1817)
CHILDHOOD

If I had a childhood, it was before
I could remember. At six or seven,
enslaved children shadow servants
in the Great House or farmhands
in the field. We get clothing—shoes,
stockings, two rough linen shirts,
trousers or a jacket—when put to work.
If those wear out, we go naked,
enduring cold, hungry winters.
Though fed mostly table scraps
and coarse cornmeal mush
ladled into a wooden trough,
I came running as soon as Cook called.
I scooped mush with shingles, shells,
or my hands, scarfing down my portion
before others made it disappear.

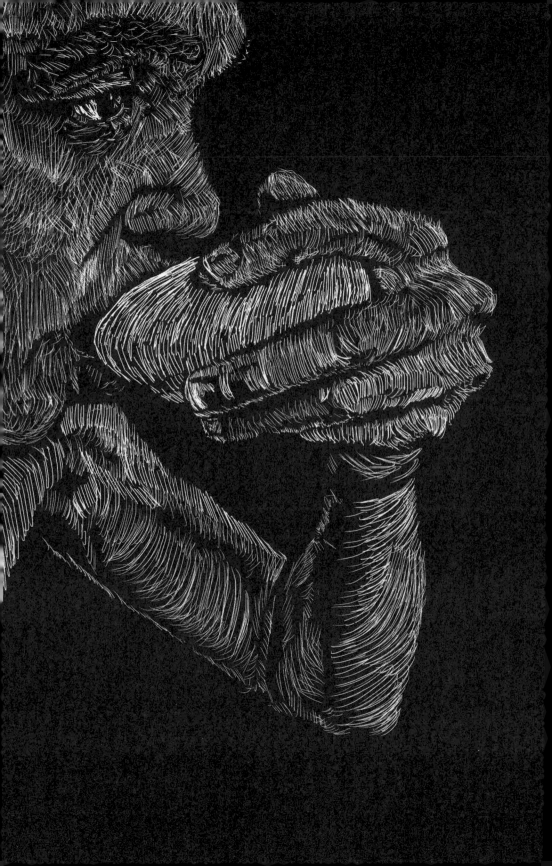

Eating fast fended off starvation.
Aromas from the kitchen made
my mouth water, my mind wander.
Does freedom taste like biscuits or cake?

The Two Pollys

POLLY COPPER SPEAKS
OF MARY TAYLOE "POLLY" LLOYD
(1784–1859)

We both named Polly.

Except my name gets called most often.

Polly, dust this.

Polly, scrub that.

Polly, fetch this.

Polly, Polly, all day long!

Miss Polly gets called too—

to lessons and supper and sewing circles.

We was both reared in the Great House.

Started as playmates.

Now, we mistress and servant.

Miss Polly ain't been herself

since the lawyer Mister Key

give her that slip of paper.

He penned a love poem for me, she gushed.
If she's read those verses once,
she's read them a dozen times.

I can't read a lick,
but I know the poem means
that Mister Francis Scott Key
intends to ask Colonel Lloyd
for Miss Polly's hand in marriage
and she will be leaving Wye House.
I pray she won't take me with her.
I couldn't bear to leave my folks.

Francis Scott Key
THE LAND OF THE FREE
AND THE HOME OF THE ENSLAVED

When Polly and I married,

we did not expect that fame would find us.

I would have practiced law in obscurity

and been known only as a second-rate poet

had I not written "The Star-Spangled Banner"

while viewing the Battle of Fort McHenry

from the Baltimore harbor in 1814.

I paired my patriotic lyrics with a melody

borrowed from a drinking ditty.

Like Polly, I was born into a slaveholding family,

bred to look down on African descendants.

But I am of two minds about the slavery.

On one hand, I enslaved Blacks in my household.

In my lifetime, I freed seven of them,

including Clem, whom I now pay wages

to supervise my plantation.

I fought against the transatlantic slave trade

and volunteered to represent enslaved
and free Blacks in the courts.
For that I am called "a friend of men of color."

Yet I defend the rights of enslavers
to recapture their possessions.
I prosecute abolitionists for aiding runaways
and for publishing positions that could incite revolts.

And I objected to the British offer
of freedom to enslaved men who joined
their attack on the United States in the War of 1812.
Indeed, my anthem proclaimed:
No refuge could save the hireling and slave
From the terror of flight or the gloom of the grave,
And the star-spangled banner in triumph doth wave
O'er the land of the free and the home of the brave.

But I did not want to deny the Black man freedom.
On the contrary. As a founder
of the American Colonization Society,
I advocate returning African descendants to Africa.

When a case I tried sparked a race riot,
I stood at the jail door to stop a lynch mob
from hanging an enslaved eighteen-year-old
accused of trying to kill his mistress.

The sun shines on me. But behind the curtain
of slavery, my views could not be cloudier.

THE KEY TO
Patriotism

Born in Baltimore, the same city
as "The Star-Spangled Banner,"
I knew the name of poet Francis Scott Key
before I did those of my own ancestors.
Hands over hearts, my third-grade class
practiced the national anthem's
first verse until we memorized it.
The high notes strained
even young vocal cords.
Why attempt more verses?
As if a reward, a field trip
capped our study of local history.

Fort McHenry had not yet been declared
a national shrine, but visits there
were already a Baltimore ritual.
In the 1960s, when some places still barred
Blacks, my family had outings there.

The fort's fifteen cannons guarded the harbor—
then among the young nation's busiest ports.
With fifteen stars and stripes—each two feet tall—
the flag that inspired Key to write his famous poem
measured thirty by forty-two feet—a size
meant to make British invaders think twice.
Mary Pickersgill toiled seven weeks—
with help from her daughter and two nieces
and Grace, a thirteen-year-old Black indentured
servant—stitching the woolen banner.

At the National Museum of American History,
I saw that flag in all its tattered glory.
Battle-worn, threadbare, fabric
full of holes—like the biased history
that I was fed. Five decades later,
I would learn that the anthem's
third verse undergirds slavery.
Frayed symbols unravel,
revealing threads of truth.

Isaac Copper II
(BORN 1798)
FREE SOLES

My uncles Jacob and Matt Copper
taught me the shoemaking craft:
how to make patterns, cut leather,
and stretch uppers onto a last with pliers,
how to punch holes with an awl
and stitch uppers and soles together.

How many shoes do we make a year?
Multiply the number of enslaved by two.
For each farmhand, a winter allotment
of one pair of straight-lasted country shoes.
The shoes take about two hours to make
and last five weeks. When those shoes
wear out, we go barefoot in the cold.
Sometimes, I stash shoes for brave souls
plotting escape. When they flee,
part of me goes too, spiriting them north.

John Copper
(BORN C. 1831)
CULTIVATING KNOWLEDGE

I grew up with Edward Lloyd VI.

As boys, we oystered on Bruff's Island.

I never had a day of schooling.

What I know comes from reading.

Young Master started me off, learning

alphabets, words, and sentences.

Before long, I was sneaking books

to the garden where I'd hide for hours

despite laws that barred

enslaved people from reading and writing.

Between the boxwoods and the beans,

the seed of resistance took root.

Jenny Whispers

I have heard of a way Underground
to outwit the patrollers and hounds.
A conductor named Moses
mines lore, codes, and poses.
Her freedom train's chugging northbound.

Harriet Tubman: Moses

I.

Whenever I go back home for my kin,

to lead them to freedom, others beg

to come too. They ache to escape.

Who am I not to show them the way?

Yet, for every passenger I bring on board,

the risk to my band rises by one.

November 1856.

Pop tells me that Josiah Bailey,

kin to Frederick Douglass,

had sent a message.

Next time Moses comes,

let me know. I'm ready to go.

A timber foreman for a shipbuilder,

Josiah heard he'd soon be sold.

For complaining, he was stripped

and whipped buck naked.

That lash virtually scrawled a map

to the Promised Land on Josiah's back.

But he had neither a mirror

nor eyes in the back of his head.

All he knew deep in his bones:

He had to set himself free.

That was more than a month ago.

II.

From Reverend Samuel Green's house

in East New Market, I lead Josiah, Peter, and Eliza

from Maryland to northern Delaware.

They hide in stationmaster Thomas Garrett's

farmhouse near the bridge to Pennsylvania.

On a wagon, the three runaways, hidden

beneath bricks and tools, envision

building new lives. From Philadelphia,

they head to Canada to avoid capture

under the Fugitive Slave Act. Josiah's owner

advertised a fifteen-hundred-dollar reward for his capture,

the most ever on the Eastern Shore.

The price on my head rose too—

from twenty to forty thousand dollars.

No one got a dime for none of us.

Emory Roberts: Runaway

(AS REPORTED IN *THE UNDERGROUND RAILROAD* BY WILLIAM STILL)

I flee Wye House in spring of 1855,

without my mother, brothers, and sisters.

Far as I know, they are still Lloyd property.

My wife was hired out to another plantation.

I leave her, too. That keeps me up nights.

That June, I reached Philadelphia,

hungry, in rags; no arms greeting me

save William Still of the Anti-Slavery Society.

He writes in his book, as I state my name,

former home, and previous condition.

My master, Colonel Lloyd,

would just as soon flog a woman

as a man, a child as an adult.

The lash was as frequent as food.

I no longer worry about the whip,

but I already miss my dear wife.

Frederick Douglass
"MEN OF COLOR, TO ARMS!"

[T]he arm of the slave . . . [is] the best defense against the arm of the slaveholder.

I have implored the imperiled nation to unchain against her foes, her powerful black hand.

I urge you to fly to arms.

The iron gate of our prison stands half open. One gallant rush from the North will fling it wide open, while four millions of our brothers and sisters shall march out into liberty. The chance is now given you to end in a day the bondage of centuries, and to rise in one bound from social degradation to the plane of common equality. . . .

Matthew Roberts
FROM RUNAWAY TO SOLDIER

Before the overseer makes good

on his threat to whip me,

I run from Wye to the next farm.

Men on horseback hunt me like game.

I run from field to field, farm to farm.

At the creek, I throw my hat in

and let it sail out to make my pursuers

think that I have crossed to the other side.

Then I return to the shoreline

and hide in wild grapevines.

The men, so close I hear them say:

He's gone overboard. He drowned himself.

No use looking for him. Their chase ends.

Later, I walk to Miles River Bridge

and ride a steamer to Baltimore.

The Union Army is recruiting there,

and I join the U.S. Colored Troops.

My Question
FOR THE LOOKING GLASSES

Once, my ancestors' reflections
were in these mirrors in place of mine.
The mirrors saw their wholeness,
even if enslavement diminished it.

You favor someone, the mirror notes.

Looking glasses everywhere at Wye,
their number grew from three
in 1685 to six in 1697 to eight in 1719.
Eventually, two in the hall chamber.
Three in Henrietta Maria's upstairs quarters.
An expensive one painted with gilt designs
to match a dresser and tea table,
all imitating Chinese lacquered furniture.
One surrounded by gilded beading.
A mahogany one.
Two with gilded frames.
A pair of thirteen-footers—in their day,

a set of four and among the longest
continuous mirrors in the land—
illuminate the North Parlor.
The tall looking glasses, now desilvered
with age and veiled with dark splotches;
brilliance fading like firsthand memories.

Those mirrors witnessed young masters'
mischief, gentleman's agreements,
ladies' sewing circles, contrivances,
conflicts, and contradictions,
flickering candles, and gleaming eyes.

My ancestors' faces in succession.

Seen but not heard at suppers
and soirees and unable to turn
a blind eye to slavery—
the looking glass remains forever
neutral as generations dart past
or pose to ponder reflections;
each scene as fleeting as the last.

Fixed with portraits on the walls,
mirrors in the rooms and halls
see the well dressed off to balls.
Mirror, mirror on the wall:
Who's the fairest Lloyd of all?
Did any dare, for fairness, call?

Mirrors are stuck in reverse.
Clocks are better measures.
Time will tell.

Timepiece

Tick tock, tick tock.
Tall Wooden Case Clock.
Crafted by English clockmakers for Edward Lloyd II,
my eight-day movement dates to 1720 at the latest.
Edward IV replaced my original case with this one.
I have stood in this hall since the late nineteenth century.

Tick tock, tick tock.
French Ormolu Clock.
Sometime after Edward Lloyd V hosted
the Maryland visit of the Marquis de Lafayette
in 1824, I arrived from France adorned
with wheat-farming motifs denoting
the Lloyds' vocation, and a fire gilded finish,
fitting the family's status among planters.
I exemplify the ormolu technique.
A paste of pure gold—pounded
and ground—and liquid mercury
was brushed on my surface and heated

in a furnace, melting away the mercury
and leaving only the gold plating.
The vapors released, so toxic
that French gilders suffered dementia
and rarely reached forty years of age.
France barred the process around 1830.
I am precious indeed. Even more so,
as a reputed gift from the marquis.

At the time, my price tag was higher
than that for an enslaved adult
whose time was not their own.

Tick tock, tick tock.
Slavery, a headlock.
Tick tock, tick tock.

Isaac Copper III

Like the Isaac Coppers who came before me,

I am a servant in the Great House.

For a century, Lloyds called Coppers their property.

I have had two masters, Edward the VI and VII,

when a Union officer shows up at Wye House

in September 1863. He demands

one hundred fit Black men.

As soon as I hear, I volunteer.

The officer pays Colonel Lloyd

three hundred dollars a head—

not the market price of fifteen hundred—

for each man freed to join the Union Army.

We march with the officer to Easton Point.

Though the colonel is an enslaver losing part

of his birthright, he follows us to the wharf;

tells us to serve the army as well as we had him.

On board the ship bound for Baltimore, I feel
the burdens of bondage alight from my chest
like geese taking wing from the banks of the Wye.
The weight that my ancestors bore, replaced
by possibilities and a purpose that I picked.
The Chesapeake Bay is wider than I imagined.
I am free—at least to fight for liberty.

MY FIRST GLIMMER OF
Isaac Copper III

The reference librarian could not draw a line
from Doctor Isaac Copper of Wye House
to my great-great-grandfather Isaac.
To me, the latter Isaac was a headstone,
the village he settled and the war he won.
But no hint of his likeness
until the librarian
fetched his military records.
The company rolls gave me a glimmer
of the man and of his march to freedom.

C 7 U.S.C.T.

Isaac Cooper

_____, Co. E, 7 Reg't U.S. Col'd Inf.

Appears on

Company Descriptive Book

of the organization named above.

DESCRIPTION

Age 20 years; height 5 feet 5½ inches

Complexion Black

Eyes Black; Hair Curly

Where born Kent, Md.

Occupation Farmer

ENLISTMENT

When Sept 24 1863

Where Baltimore

*By whom Col Wm
Birney; term 3 y'rs.*

*Remarks: In the
engagement
on John's Island in
S.C. July 9 1864*

**Ahhh. His eyes
were black.
He was born
around 1843.**

C | *7* | **U.S.C.T**

Isaac Cooper

.............., Co. **C**., 7 Reg't U.S. Col'd In

Appears on

Company Descriptive Book

of the organization named above.

DESCRIPTION.

Age 20 years; height 5 feet 5½ inches

Complexion Black

Eyes Black ; hair Curly

Where born Kent, Md.

Occupation Farmer

ENLISTMENT.

When Sept 24, 186 3.

Where Baltimore

By whom Col Wm Birney ; term 3 y'rs.

Remarks: In the engagement on John's Island, S.C. July 9, 1864.

John Copper

Rumor is that I shot off my finger

during the Civil War to avoid combat.

A soldier who cannot fire a gun

is not worth his uniform buttons.

If I have only nine digits left,

it is not for lack of courage,

but because I committed

to take the future into my hands.

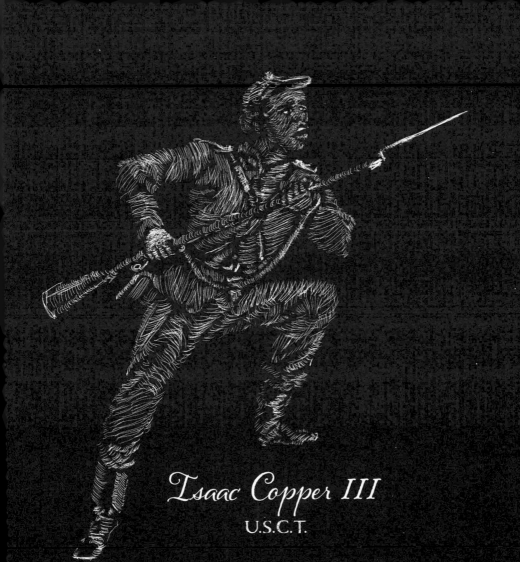

Isaac Copper III
U.S.C.T.

We train at Camp Stanton in Benedict, Maryland.

Winter on the Patuxent River claims many men.

Whether we were free or formerly enslaved,

the colored infantry is the last in line

for uniforms. Some soldiers have no boots—

just the worn shoes they walked in with.

Lacking weapons, my regiment drills
with sticks and whatever else we find.

Though I grew up watching sailboats,
schooners, and skipjacks on the Wye River,
I have never spent so much time on the water.
In March 1864, we take steamers to Portsmouth, Virginia,
and to Hilton Head, South Carolina,
and by the SS *Delaware* to Jacksonville, Florida.
We fought off the Confederates from our camp
and had several skirmishes before an expedition
on foot to the North Edisto River to break enemy lines.
Seventeen days, constant fighting, countless casualties.
Then another steamer up St. Johns River
to Black Creek to cut the railroad line at Trail Ridge,
so the rebels couldn't ship supplies by train.
After a four-month campaign at Bermuda Hundred
and a snowy Virginia winter, we marched
for weeks across the Appomattox and James Rivers
and were among the first Union troops
into the center of Petersburg as the city fell.

Our siege had broken rebel lines, leaving Richmond,
the Confederate capital, defenseless.
As Richmond burned, I was in the trenches—
reading signals of freedom in the smoky sky.
In the war's last days, we chased Lee's army
to Appomattox, where he surrendered to Grant.
Inscribed on our colors—the battles we fought:
Appomattox Court House, Armstrong's Mill,
Baldwin, Cedar Creek, Darbytown Road,
Fort Gilmer, Fussell's Mill, Johns Island,
New Market Heights, Petersburg, and White Point.
These ghosts sleep with me every night:
eighty-five men lost in battle and 308 to disease.
After the war, a steamship to Indianola, Texas,
to serve garrison duty as cholera raged.

I hear that the 7th Regiment traveled more
than most other Civil War units;
a journey not in miles, knots, or days,
but in footsteps to freedom.
I am turning my feet toward home.

Isaac Copper III
FOUNDING FATHER OF UNIONVILLE

I left the Eastern Shore as property

and return a freeman at the doorway

to the dream that I have dreamed forever.

With not so much as a roof over my head,

I head to Wye House to fetch my family.

Still working as if the war never was.

A rough start. Sharecropping until 1867.

Then, with seventeen other veterans,

I enter a contract with Ezekiel Cowgill,

a Quaker who owns Lombardy.

He agrees to carve a piece of his plantation

for us to start a town, if we will build

a school and a church. The lease:

eighteen of us must pay

one dollar a year for thirty years.

When short on cash for rent,

we work off our debts.

At first, we call our village

Cowgilltown, but folks soon call it
Unionville—in our honor.
For two dollars, we buy land
for a school and St. Stephen's A.M.E. Church.
Unionville grows to nearly forty buildings.
Me and my wife, Susan, raise our daughters,
Mary and Elizabeth, in the home
we built ourselves. My offspring
will learn to read, write, and cypher,
and will bow to *no* man—only to God.

John Copper Returns

First, I was enslaved at Wye House—
a boyhood friend to Edward Lloyd VI.
I learned to read as a boy, but I
    couldn't write.
Then, I was a servant in the
    Great House.
When word spread that I
    had a good mind,
other enslaved people
    sought my advice.

After serving in the U.S. Colored Troops

during the Civil War, I went up to Delaware

and worked on a small farm for a man

that nobody else could get along with.

I didn't stay away from Talbot County long.

When I came back, I put down roots

not far from Wye House. We named

our village Liberty. But soon

it was called Copperville.

I owned my own land and a fishing boat

and was my own boss. A waterman,

I tonged oysters. Wasn't much money,

but it was mine. I earned it honest.

Growing Up in Unionville

Roosters crowed each new morning,
children roamed fields, played hopscotch
and hide-and-seek, and slid down
straw stacks after the wheat harvest.
They bought caramels and peppermints
from the Greene or Copper stores,
and along the roadside, they picked
wild blueberries and asparagus.

The homes had wells and outhouses,
and kerosene-lit parlors—no electricity
or indoor plumbing. Yet faith and hope
flowed freely; the church, a balm
for the backache of segregation.

Only one resident had a telephone—
a party line that she let neighbors use.
Even without phones, news traveled fast,
rumors and gossip spreading like vines.

Miz Sophie picked peonies for children
to give to their mamas.
And if a child down the road cut up,
word reached home before they did.

Once, Unionville School made news.
During the Great Depression,
the board of education ordered
that the whites-only McDaniel School building
be moved to Unionville. The school
came overland on wheels, was pulled
onto a custom-built scow, tugged
to Miles River Bridge, put ashore,
and hauled a mile down Unionville Road.
The next spring, we had a Maypole.

Teachers did their best to fill in the gaps
of separate but unequal education.
Before copy machines, they handwrote
worksheets for every student in class.
They cultivated students sure as grown folks
did the fields: lessons in the three R's

and respect mixed with rules to live by.

On the classroom's pot-bellied stove,

the teacher simmered soup, oatmeal, and cocoa;

school, an arm of home.

Renting rooms from residents,

the teachers were always nearby.

Isaac Copper III
GARDENER, 1920

I have been free now longer than I was enslaved:
free to marry Susan and put down roots in Unionville,
free to attend church and send my daughters to school,
free to decide what wisdom to guard and what to give away.

If a plant grows above ground, sow
when the moon is waxing; if below
ground, when the moon is waning.

Charged with the garden at Hope, I waited
on the moon and raised crops by the stars.
Missus Starr was amazed that I knew where storms
were moving and that I prayed for rain.

Rain pours when the crescent moon stands upright.

Of beets, cabbage, cauliflower, carrots, potatoes,
I am proudest of making flowers sing.

Missus Starr was grateful for the Black hands
that tended her heart-shaped garden.

Never let the May sun on a June bean.

In 1925, she dedicated Memorial Day
to the colored citizens of Talbot County.
Her notice in the *Star Democrat* invited
the entire Black community to a garden party.

Don't plant your corn until the dogwood storms.

At Hope House, those that could write
signed the leather-bound guest book,
names filling three pages. I was guest of honor.
That was one fine celebration!

An acorn in the pocket blesses the harvest.

Two Markers

Two historical markers go up
on the two-lane country road:
one commemorating the village
of Unionville and the other listing
the community's founders, eighteen
African American Civil War veterans—
formerly enslaved and free Blacks who fought
in the U.S. Colored Troops and are buried
behind St. Stephen's A.M.E. Church.
On Memorial Day, flags mark vets' graves.
Weather has wiped clean a few
of the slim limestone grave markers.
Others lean a bit, like weary soldiers.
But Isaac Copper's stands at attention.

THE FOREST, THE TREES,
the Royal Roots

One acorn can grow a tree and seed a forest.
Or a family tree.

I never met any of these relatives
but my late father grew up among them.
Nor had I heard of Ruth Starr Rose, who was born
in Wisconsin but spent her teens at Hope House.
How amazing that a socialite like Rose
chose to paint my rural kin during the 1930s
rather than wealthy white subjects.
Her models, Unionville and Copperville folk,
were among Maryland's founding families,
said the collector who curated the exhibit.
I saw my kin in a blinding new light.

Browsing the exhibition catalog at home,
I notice an old photograph
of Rose's parents' gardener, Isaac Copper.

He lived in Unionville and was crowned
the "Royal Black" because he could trace
his lineage to African royalty.
Though I can pinpoint neither tribe
nor nation of origin, I am content
with this lore and with my discovery.
I never dreamed that I would see
my great-great-grandfather's face.

Questions remain,
but this knowledge
is more than I could ask.

The tree grows tall and strong.

A Tale of Two Statues

(IN THREE VOICES)

Frederick Douglass	Common Soldier, to the Talbot Boys

In the Civil War, Maryland was a border state, neither seceding from the Union nor advocating slavery's abolition. Three hundred of Talbot County's sons fought for the Union and ninety-two for the Confederacy. Cousin against cousin.

Decoration Day speech, 1878.
There was a right side and a wrong side
in the late war, which no sentiment
ought to cause us to forget,
and while today we should have malice
toward none, and charity toward all,
it is no part of our duty to confound right
with wrong, or loyalty with treason.

1916. With a Confederate flag unfurling over my shoulder, I marched onto the Talbot County courthouse lawn at the height of the segregation era. Fifty years after the Civil War ended, and a year after *The Birth of a Nation* glorified the Ku Klux Klan and became the first movie screened at the White House. Like that three-hour epic, I am silent. I was erected by Citizens After War. No masterpiece, I was mass-produced. Mullins Sheet Metal of Salem, Ohio, stocked a ready supply of life-size common soldiers made of copper. For decades, I had this lawn all to myself.

Frederick Douglass	Narrator	Common Soldier, to the Talbot Boys

My road to immortality passes through
Route 33, which connects Easton to St.
Michaels. In 2009, after much controversy,
that highway is dedicated to me.

A few years later, Talbot County debates a
statue of me, a once-enslaved Black man, for
the courthouse green. The county council
rules that my monument can be no taller
than the Talbot boy. I 2011, a crane hoists
my bronze likeness onto a granite plinth.
The sculptor depicted me in mid-sentence,
my right hand raised to stress a point. At
my unveiling, two ministers, one Black and
one white, pour a libation, calling ancestral
spirits. Choirs sing and dignitaries speak. On
lampposts, sepia-toned banners: "Douglass
Returns." "Triumphant," I might add.

In 2020, the battle of historical memory
reignites after a white police officer
suffocates George Floyd, an unarmed Black
man in Minneapolis. Across the country,
calls for justice and to remove Confederate
symbols.

Frederick Douglass	Narrator	Common Soldier, to the Talbot Boys

The last such icon on Maryland state
property. I tire of lifting the colors of
defeat. The burden, too heavy to bear.
Local civil rights groups sue to evict
me from the only home I have ever
known.

On roadsides and front lawns,
Dueling signs in yellow and blue:
"Remove Talbot's Confederate Statue"
and "Preserve Talbot Heritage."

I have been on this podium ten years
when county leaders sense the tide
turning. They want to part ways with the
Talbot boy.

But no one wants me, not even
the cemetery, preferring to bury
the Lost Cause. I am a relic
engendering more ill will
than I have ever been worth.

A Black attorney boldly asks:
How can Black defendants expect
a fair trial inside a courthouse
with that symbol of oppression outside?

DOUGLASS

Frederick Douglass	Narrator	Common Soldier, *to the Talbot Boys*
		2021. Chin up, hat tipped back, I have stood guard over one hundred years atop a wagon wheel on my granite pedestal.
	Days after the Richmond, Virginia, statue of General Robert E. Lee is removed and dismantled,	
		the county council finds a resting place for me: a battlefield in Harrison, Virginia.
Now, I alone guard liberty on the county courthouse lawn. Somewhere in my long shadow		
	is the light that we seek.	

189

The Lloyd Family Cemetery

Trees and tall shrubs border a brick wall
with a pointed archway leading to
a quarter-acre family graveyard.
There lie rows of departed
Edward Lloyds and their wives
all flanking Colonel Philemon Lloyd
who died in 1685 at age thirty-nine,
leaving three sons, seven daughters,
and a wife, Henrietta Maria.
A few Lloyd children died young.

For these headstones, slabs, and obelisks,
sandstone and marble were mined
from the same Aquia, Virginia, quarry
as blocks for the Capitol and White House.
Carved on the monuments: crosses,
lilies of the valley, a bouquet,
an acanthus leaf wreath,
an anchor for naval service,

the lions rampant on the Lloyd crest,

and inverted torches symbolizing

lives extinguished. Some names

on gothic-topped marble markers

barely legible, but Lloyds nonetheless.

The Key to Wye House

Lain across my palms,
the original key to Wye House
is a lead weight that still works
after being passed down
for eleven generations.

My hands tingle at the notion
that my kin held this same key
to the front door of this house
they could tend but never own.
Could a key unlock my past?

At least I have opened the door.

The Grove

I cross the newly cut cornfield
to a circular stand of trees.
At the outer rim, a bronze plaque
atop a brick pedestal marks
the final resting place of the enslaved.

IN THIS HALLOWED GROUND LIE THOSE
WHO WORKED THE PLANTATION OF
WYE HOUSE FROM ITS BEGINNING
1665 – CIRCA – 1900
ERECTED BY THE LLOYD FAMILY 1980

Tracing the tribute, I read the brutal truths
between the lines of the epitaph.
This grove is halfway between
the riverbank and the Long Green—
home to hundreds of enslaved people.

I walk toward a wide tree in the center
of the circle. The midday sun beams

a welcome through the towering canopy.

The ancestors have been waiting for you.

Did Minister Isaac Copper preach here by moonlight?

Kneeling in the shade, I touch the grass.

The number buried here is unknown;

        their names, lost but for ledgers

          of the Lloyds' property and possessions.

        No more proof needed.

         Here, I feel the spirits.

            I leave a bouquet

              of cornflowers and words;

              tears flow as I pray that my kin

              are finally free.

              I am blessed that their souls

              now breathe in me.

AUTHOR'S NOTE

Growing up, I knew of only one formerly enslaved ancestor—Phillip Moaney, a co-founder of the all-Black village of Copperville. Phillip's oval portrait hung in the farmhouse built by his son and my great-grandfather, James Henry Moaney.

I was grown by the time that I learned of another great-great-grandfather, Isaac Copper. He fought in the U.S. Colored Troops and co-founded the nearby all-Black village of Unionville, where a historical marker now commemorates his contributions.

However, I did yet not grasp the full meaning of my ancestors' achievements: During Reconstruction on Maryland's Eastern Shore, my newly emancipated kin emerged from slavery to become founding fathers.

Despite these clues to family history, researching my genealogy seemed daunting. For years, I set the task aside. Then Frederick Douglass's autobiography, set partially at Wye House—Maryland's largest slaveholding plantation—sparked my curiosity. The formerly enslaved abolitionist described an Isaac Copper. Noting that enslaved people rarely had surnames, Douglass added that Isaac, a healer and minister, was also given the honorific title of Doctor. Though Douglass dreaded the switches Isaac used in teaching children to pray, he considered him a good man.

Could that Isaac Copper have been my great-great-grandfather? Although Douglass could forgive the switches, I could not. For years, I stopped digging. I began anew when this project formed in my mind.

The trail tracing my family's past and narrating their truths was meandering. One discovery did not immediately lead to another. Nor did facts come to light in chronological order. I succeeded in connecting some dots, but gaps remain.

My quest took me to the Maryland Historical Society, the Talbot County Free Library, the Talbot County Historical Society, the Library of Congress, and to the wrought iron gates of that plantation—Wye House. I read archeological and anthropological studies of the plantation. I searched databases of slave ships and of the enslaved residents of Wye House. I saw my ancestors' names inked on plantation ledgers and military records. I got wind of family lore claiming ties to African royalty. But like the genealogical searches of many African Americans with roots in slavery, my family tree went dark after five generations.

I wrote many of these poems on my family's farmstead in rural Copperville. I asked my ancestors to speak to, and through, me. These poems conjure their voices. You hear not only from my ancestors, but also from others in the enslaved community. You hear from freedom fighters Frederick Douglass and Harriet Tubman. You hear from an archeologist, the plantation owners, Wye House itself, and the Chesapeake Bay. I sometimes interrupt to pose questions that still beg for answers.

A year before conceiving this project, Jeffery and I toured schools in West Africa. Even then, my soul was searching. I pray that *Kin* honors our ancestors.

ILLUSTRATOR'S NOTE

$\mathcal{I}$ *remember* being a young boy, exploring the back roads of Copperville with my sister early in the mornings on our bicycles, the wind rushing by our faces. I recall reeling in my first snapping turtle out of our family pond. Catching my first catfish. Meeting my cousins. Picking blueberries with my mother while dew was still on the grass. Seeing bald eagles fly and perch on tall trees overlooking our cornfield. I remember reading the historical markers that tell the story of Unionville's origin and looking across the road at the little yellow one-room schoolhouse that my grandfather attended as a boy.

I created this body of illustrations to help tell the story of my ancestors. I have an obligation to them to spread their story to the people so that others may be inspired to explore their roots and reclaim their history—the good, the bad, and the ugly. It is a call to future artists to stay dedicated to the process and stay in tune with their "why." *Kin* is a love note to perseverance, to everyone who has had to endure pain silently in any way, shape, or form. I hope that these illustrations inspire those who view them to be great.

BIBLIOGRAPHY

Academy Art Museum and Frederick Douglass Honor Society. Douglass Returns (pamphlet). 2011.

Baradel, Lacey. "History of Early American Landscape Design: Wye House." National Gallery of Art, Center for Advanced Studies in the Visual Arts. heald.nga.gov/mediawiki/index.php/Wye_House.

Blight, David W. *Frederick Douglass: Prophet of Freedom*. New York: Simon & Schuster, 2020.

Bolden, Tonya. *Tell All the Children Our Story: Memories and Mementos of Being Young and Black in America*. New York: Harry N. Abrams Inc., 2002.

Callum, Agnes Kane. *Colored Volunteers of the Maryland Civil War: 7th Regiment United States Colored Troops, 1863–1866*. Baltimore: Mullac Publishers, 1990.

Department of Anthropology at the University of Maryland, College Park, and Historic Annapolis Foundation. Archaeology in Annapolis Project. "People of Wye House." Database. aia.umd.edu/.

Douglass, Frederick. "Men of Color, To Arms!" rbscp.lib.rochester.edu/4372.

Douglass, Frederick and William Lloyd Garrison. *Narrative of the Life of Frederick Douglass, an American Slave*. Boston: Anti-Slavery Office, 1849. Retrieved from the Library of Congress, loc.gov/item/82225385/.

Equal Justice Initiative. "Black Families Severed by Slavery." eji.org/news/history-racial-injustice-black-families-severed-by-slavery/.

Kast, Sheilah, and Maureen Harvie. "Frederick Douglass and the Enslaved People of Wye House." WYPR podcast, *On the Record*.

https://www.wypr.org/show/on-the-record/2017-04-26/frederick
-douglass-and-the-enslaved-people-of-wye-house.

La Prade, Joy. "History No Longer Buried." *Star Democrat*. August 27,
2006. stardem.com/news/article_41daf44d-5c87-5671-b1a9
-237ceecceaca.html.

Lloyd Family and Maryland Historical Society. *The Lloyd Papers:
Manuscript 2001 in the Maryland Historical Society, Baltimore.*
Wilmington, Del: Scholarly Resources, Inc., 1972.

Maryland Genealogy Trails. "Anne Arundel County Maryland Colonial
Families: Lloyd." genealogytrails.com/mary/annearundel
/colonialfamilies_Lloyd.html.

Maryland Historical Trust. "T-934: Easton Confederate Monument."
mht.maryland.gov/secure/medusa/pdf/talbot/t-934.pdf.

The Maryland State Archives and the University of Maryland, College
Park. "A Guide to the History of Slavery in Maryland." msa
.maryland.gov/msa/intromsa/pdf/slavery_pamphlet.pdf.

Nery, Steve. "Md. Route 33 Gets Douglass Designation." *Star Democrat*.
March 29, 2009. stardem.com/news/md-route-33-gets-douglass
-designation/article_c35d5993-8566-5189-aeba-534e02d352c9.html.

Paca, Barbara. *Ruth Starr Rose (1887–1965): Revelations of African
American Life in Maryland and the World.* Baltimore: Reginald
F. Lewis Museum of Maryland African American History &
Culture, 2015.

Pruitt, Elizabeth. *Reordering the Landscape of Wye House: Nature,
Spirituality, and Social Order.* Lanham, Maryland: Lexington
Books, 2017.

The Second Maryland Infantry, USA, & Maryland in the Civil War.
"7th U.S. Colored Troops." 2ndmdinfantryus.org/USCT7.html.

SlaveVoyages. Database. slavevoyages.org/.

Speckart, Amy. "The Colonial History of Wye Plantation, the Lloyd Family, and their Slaves on Maryland's Eastern Shore: Family, Property, and Power." PhD dissertation, College of William & Mary, 2011. scholarworks.wm.edu/cgi/viewcontent.cgi?article =3371&context=etd.

Stauffer, John, Zoe Trodd, and Celeste-Marie Bernier. *Picturing Frederick Douglass: An Illustrated Biography of the Nineteenth Century's Most Photographed American.* New York: W. W. Norton & Company, 2015.

Tinker, Steve and Clio Admin. "Wye House." Clio: Your Guide to History. Last modified February 29, 2020. theclio.com/entry/95796.

Twitty, Michael W. "Food on a Maryland Plantation: Frederick Douglass Speaks." *Afroculinaria.* July 18, 2014. afroculinaria.com/2014/07/18 /food-on-a-maryland-plantation-frederick-douglass-speaks.

University of Maryland, Department of Anthropology. "Frederick Douglass and Wye House: Archeology and African-American Culture in Maryland." anth.umd.edu/feature/frederick-douglass -and-wye-house-archaeology-and-african-american-culture -maryland.

Willis, Deborah. *The Black Civil War Soldier: A Visual History of Conflict and Citizenship.* New York: New York University Press, 2021.

Wolf II, Edwin. "The Library of Edward Lloyd IV of Wye House." *Winterthur Portfolio 5* (1969): see p. 92–121.

Wood, Peter H. *Strange New Land: Africans in Colonial America.* New York: Oxford University Press, 2003.

Ydiste, John. "Plantation Dig Reveals Md. Town's Painful Past." NPR. https://www.npr.org/transcripts/15383164.